He Saved Me.

....

Susie Ferguson

Contents

o n e	1
t w o	6
t h r e e	11
f o u r	16
f i v e	21
chapter six	24
chapter seven	28
chapter eight	31
chapter nine	35
chapter ten	38
chapter eleven	42
chapter twelve	46
chapter thirteen	49
chapter fourteen	55
chapter fifteen	59

chapter sixteen 65

chapter seventeen 69

chapter eighteen 76

chapter nineteen 83

chapter twenty 88

chapter twenty one 94

chapter twenty two 99

chapter twenty three 105

chapter twenty four 111

chapter twenty five 116

chapter twenty six 120

chapter twenty seven 123

o n e

I looked down at my phone and hesitated dialing his number. My brother left so long ago I haven't talked to him forever but there was no way I could stay here.

I had just gotten my acceptance letter, which was the only sign I needed to leave my boyfriend Cade.

I had been putting up with his abuse for years thinking he would change and would become the man I thought I had started a relationship with but he never did he blamed me for everything.

A part of me thinks maybe I deserved it. If I was just a better girlfriend if I did more for him he wouldn't beat me. But no matter what I do I'll never be good enough for him so I needed to leave before things got even worst.

I swallowed back my anxiety and dialed my brothers number. I held my breath waiting for him to pick up he finally did. "Hey" I froze hearing his voice. "Hello anyone there?"

"Umm Jake it's uhh it's Madison." "Oh uhhh Madison hey how are you?" "I'm ok I uhhh I had a question well a big favor I needed to ask." I hesitate.

"Alright shoot." " I was wondering if I could umm come stay with you..." silence no answer I swallowed back the urge to just hangup and started rambling. "I'm so sorry to ask this I really am I don't want to impose it's just I just got accepted to NYU and I umm I really need to leave as soon as possible I can't ummm." My voice breaks and I scream at myself in my head I hated sounding so weak I hated having to plead with someone.

"I'm sorry this was stupid never mind." I go to Hangup but before I can I hear his voice. "Mads of course you can please come whenever you need to you're always welcome." "Really?" My voice breaks even more.

"Yes please come I'd love to see you." "Thank you Jake thank you so much you have no idea what this means to me."

"No problem just shoot me a text when you figure out the date." "I uhhh was actually planning on trying to book a flight tomorrow if that's not too soon I'm really sorry to inconvenience you I know school doesn't start for a few months, I just I can't stay in California any longer for reasons I should probably explain later but I just uhhh I I really have to leave but if that's too soon it's ok." I pause.

"No you're not an inconvenience that's completely fine." I smile we talk a little more and then hangup. I'm actually getting out of here.

I started packing my duffel bag stuffing whatever I could in. Any furniture I had would have to stay otherwise Cade would get suspicious. Just then I heard the door open I quickly ran and shoved my duffel bag under the bed in our guest room.

I suddenly heard glass shatter I froze and then remembered the acceptance letter, I had left it on the counter Fuck.

I felt my legs start to tremble I knew what was about to happen. I quickly shut the door. I wish I could've locked it but Cade got rid of the locks a long time ago.

I ran to our closet and hid behind some clothes I prayed he would not be able to find me, but I knew he would he always did. I hear the footsteps coming closer and closer my whole body trembling now.

Suddenly the doors were yanked open. I shut my eyes but I could feel his presence right in front of me. I could hear his heavy breathing. My hands and legs trembling in anticipation of whats about to happen.

My heart is racing I close my eyes and try and take deep breaths. I'm gonna be fine, Its gonna be okay. I tell myself over and over again.

He throws the clothes off of me and grabs me by my hair yanking me out of the closet. My head throbbing from the action I try and keep the tears at bay. My emotions are a weakness. Cade hates when I'm weak.

"What the fuck is this?" He shakes the letter in my face. I try and keep the panic from showing on my face. "Baby I don't know what you're talking about. I don't know what that is." I try and shrug it off.

"Don't. fucking. lie. to. me." He says each word slowly whispering into my ear in a terrifyingly calm manor.

"You're trying to go off to college. Well I've got news for you. You're too stupid and useless for that you fucking whore." He laughs in my ear making me tremble even harder.

He moves his hand to my throat and lifts me up squeezing I try clawing at his hands but he's too strong. "You're so weak and pathetic you couldn't make it 2 days without me." He laughs in my face his breath reeks of whiskey.

He lets go of my throat letting me collapse on the ground. I curl up in a ball trying to make myself as small as possible. I feel him kick me over and over again.

The punches then start. One makes it into my face I whimper and throw my arms in front of my face. He usually avoids my face not wanting anyone to know.

I try and make my mind go somewhere else and ignore the pain but I can't I'm stuck, frozen. Finally he stops and storms out and I hear the front door slam.

****

I just lay there and once I'm sure that he's gone I let the tears come out sobs shaking my body.

I finally get the strength to try and stand up I see the acceptance letter torn to pieces on the ground. I gather it up and throw it in the bathroom trash can.

I look up and wince when I see myself in the mirror my eye is already turning an angry purple and my hair is in mats and bruises form along my neck. I pull my shirt up and see bruises forming all along my torso.

I don't let myself cry at the sight of it I have seen worst I'll be fine I tell myself and lower my shirt and take a brush to my hair.

I then quickly log into my computer and look up flights hoping that there might be one set to leave tonight.

I find one that has only one seat left set to leave at 2 am. It'll be risky but I have to leave sooner than I thought.

I finish stuffing some socks and underwear and a couple more shirts into my duffel bag. I then grab my hair brush and a couple of books from my nightstand drawer and stuff them into a backpack for my carry on. I

then start to change into some comfy clothes for the plane trip. I put on a pair of sweatpants and an oversized hoodie.

I put on some makeup. Carefully applying it over the bruises wincing at the contact.

Cade should be gone until at least 4 am since it's Friday night and he's pissed off so he'll prolly be out drinking with one of his friends until the bars close and then to his friends house to keep the party going.

I take a deep breath trying to calm my nerves my hands and legs are still shaking. My heart racing at the thought that I'm actually going to leave.

I sit on the couch and put on my favorite comfort show New Girl and wait.

t w o

- -

I look over at the clock it's current 11:30 I start grabbing my stuff and throwing it in my trunk. it'll take me about 30 minutes to get to the airport and then I'll have to get through security and everything.

I throw on a baseball cap grab my favorite fluffy blanket and then close the door behind me.

Once I get in my car and leave the driveway I take one last look at the apartment behind me and let out a shaky breath. I can do this. I'm going to be fine.

I pull over and stop at a gas station on my way and grab a cereal bar and 2 hard seltzers in hopes that it might calm my nerves. I flash my fake ID to the cashier and swipe my card.

I down one of the seltzers before putting my car in drive and open the cereal bar and eat it as I drive to the airport. The whole time I hold my breath waiting for Cade to show up and drag me back.

A ding from my phone makes me jump its a text from Cade who is most likely drunk.

Baby I'm sorry about earlier I just lost my temper.

Babe

Madison

Fucking answer me

I take a deep breath and send a text back.

It's okay baby I understand. I'm sorry to.

When I finally arrive at the airport I down my other seltzer before grabbing my bags and heading into the airport praying that Cade won't show up.

I exhale a breath of relief when I finally reach my seat on the plane and no sign of Cade. My leg is bouncing still not believing that I'm leaving.

When the plane takes off and I watch California become smaller and smaller. Tears well up in my eyes and I smile for the first time in a while. I am actually leaving he can't stop me.

I have about a 5 hour flight ahead of me so I take my blanket out of my backpack and the alcohol is starting to hit me making me loopy. I curl up and allow sleep to take over I can finally sleep in peace without fear creeping in.

I wake to a flight attendant announcing we were about to land to fasten our seatbelts. I quickly put my seatbelt on and looked down at my phone to check the time I see 32 missed calls from Cade and 27 text messages.

I swallow back my fear and try and take a deep breath trying to get my hand to stop shaking. It was currently 7:30 I wasn't sure if my brother would be awake yet but it would take me a little bit to get my luggage and everything.

Once we landed and I was safely in the airport waiting for my luggage I called my brother. I anxiously waited for him to answer I hoped he wouldn't be upset.

He answered "Mads what's up?" "Hey Jake umm I really don't want to bother you." "Your not a bother what's wrong are you ok?"

"Yeah I'm fine I just uhh something happened last night and I ended up having to leave earlier then I thought I am actually at the airport and I was wondering if there was anyway you could send me the address and I'll just call a cab or an Uber?"

"What do you mean something happened are you alright?" "Yeah I'm ok."

"Okay I'm at work right now but I'm going to send someone to pick you up alright you're not getting in an Uber alone."

"No no please don't do that it's alright I'm sorry I shouldn't have called I don't want to be an inconvenience." I cringed I hated that I was being such a burden on him.

"Mads it's fine don't worry about it I'm gonna send someone just sit tight for a hot minute." "Ok thanks Jake."

"Don't worry about it I'll text you when they're on their way." Before I could ask who he hung up.

I take a deep breath feeling completely defeated I stared at my phone for a minute scrolling through the text messages Cade had sent me my hands shaking as the messages became more and more threatening.

His name pops up again on my phone he's trying to call me. I decline the call and another text from him pops up on my phone.

I know where you are and I will find you. Don't think for a single second that you are going to get away with this. You'll never make it in New York. You're a dirty worthless disgusting whore and you won't last without me.

My hands shake and my mouth goes dry. I feel like I'm going to throw up. I quickly block his number and take a deep breath closing my eyes for a second. I then quickly looked up realizing I hadn't even been looking for my luggage. Once I find it I go and sit and wait for my brother to text me.

I must've dozed off because I jolt awake at the sound of my phone ringing. I look down to see Jake calling I pick up. "Hey." "Hey are you ok I've been texting you you never responded?"

"Yes oh my god I'm good I'm so sorry I must've dozed off."

"Oh ok well my friends Noah and Nicky are waiting outside for you they'll take you to the house and I'll be back around 6."

"Fuck I'm so sorry were they waiting long." I mentally kick myself god how could I have fallen asleep.

"No they just got here a few minutes ago you're good I can imagine you're exhausted but they said they were at the front and they're in Nicky's car so look for a white suv and text me if you can't find them." "Ok thanks Jake."

I step outside and immediately spot a white suv and start heading towards them praying it was the right car.

A young blonde who looks to be around my brothers age jumps out of the passenger seat and rushes over to me.

Startled I stumble back a little trying to hide my wince as she pulls me in for a hug. "Hi omgg you look so much like Jake I'm so happy to meet you I'm Nicky!"

Surprised by how nice she's being I freeze for a second before responding. "I uhhh I'm Madison it's so nice to meet you I'm so sorry you had to come get me."

"Oh it's no trouble at all." A tall steadily built blonde guy comes walking towards me motioning for me to give him my bag.

I hesitantly hand it over. "Thats Noah my boyfriend and I'm sure Jake has mentioned him to you those two are so close." She leans over and whispers to me so Noah can't hear her "If I wasn't his girlfriend I'd think they were gay for each other." Nicky explains.

I laugh at her and immediately feel myself relaxing.

The whole ride home Nicky talked my ear off explaining how Noah and Jake had bought the house in their name and how everyone pitches in for rent.

There was seven of them living there, Noah, Jake, Asher, Ethan, Brooke, Jules and Nicky.

Nicky subtly hinted that they had an extra room available since she had just recently moved into Noahs room and that I should stay permanently.

I got excited by the idea but I don't want to intrude on my brothers life. I hadn't seen my brother in 5 years now he didn't even come to my parents funeral but I mean I can't blame him our parents were horrible to him they weren't any better to me but he never knew that.

He moved out as soon as he turned 18 and the second he left my parents refused to let me have any contact with him. We used to be really close I missed that but now my brother has moved on built a whole other life for himself that seems amazing.

We finally pull up to a gorgeous modern looking house.

t h r e e

I followed Nicky inside, Noah following behind us carrying my duffel bag even though I insisted on carrying it myself.

Laughter echoed throughout the house. I hadn't heard that in a while. I paused at the doorway for a second I could feel my anxiety creeping in. What if none of them like me what if I've changed so much and Jake won't like me? A million thoughts rush through my head.

"Come on I'll introduce you to everyone." Nicky grabbed my arm startling me I flinch and she immediately lets go. "I'm so sorry I didn't mean to startle you you must be exhausted let me introduce you to everyone real fast and then I'll show you to your room."

I nodded afraid my voice would break if I tried to speak. She gently takes my arm and leads me closer to the sound of laughter.

I could feel the anxiety rising higher the closer I got to the sound. In the living room sat 4 more people two girls and two boys. Nicky introduced the other blonde girl as Jules and the dark haired girl as Brooke and the two boys as Asher and Ethan.

Asher didn't say a word to me just nodded his head. Ethan smiled at me and the girls stood up and each gave me a big hug.

"Oh my gosh it's so good to meet you I've been so excited to meet Jakes sister y'all looks so much alike." Jules squealed. "Jules chill you're gonna scare her." Brooke laughed, "as you can probably tell we're really happy to have you here right guys." She shot an intimidating look towards Asher and Asher just grunted in return.

"Don't mind him he hasn't gotten laid in how it long has it been a a whole day now?" Ethan stands up laughing.

Asher shoots a death glare Ethan's way and Nicky shoots a stern look towards both of them and changes the subject.

"Anyways now that these goons have basically probably scared you off let me show you to your room." Nicky leads the way shaking her head at the group of people. I

force a laugh and follow her. They all seem really nice except for Asher he doesn't seem to want me here. Even if it's just one person that doesn't want me here I refuse to be a burden so I can't stay long I stress in my mind.

(The room.... I imagined something simple but if theres another room you imagine pretend thats inserted ;))

Nicky opens the door and steps aside to let me through and Noah soon follows carrying my duffel bag and tosses it on the bed.

"Wow this is beautiful thank you." Nicky smiles "I'm so happy you like it, we'll let you rest for a little Jake should be getting home soon."

Nicky motions for Noah to follow her out the door and then shuts it behind her. I sit down on the bed and look around my mind still couldn't process that I was safe. I let myself sink into the pillows and closed my eyes.

--- Ashers Pov ---

Jake had talked to me last night about his sister. He said she was going to come stay with us but he didn't expect for a couple of days then the next thing I know his text came in the group chat saying his sister got in early and he needed someone to pick her up.

Of course Nicky was the first to volunteer her and Noah. I don't understand why nobody else was upset about this.

It's ridiculous how inconsiderate she was. It wasn't that much of an inconvenience to anyone except me.

Why? Because I had been storing a couple of my extra things in the guest room because my dad refused to keep it if I wouldn't come home to his house for the summer.

I was just going to leave it in there because I mean how did the girl expect us to be ready for her if she can't plan ahead and communicate. Nicky however begged me to get all my stuff out because she wanted it to look nice for her.

Because I can't say no to Nicky me and Ethan spent the morning clearing out the room and taking it to a storage unit instead of my original plan which was to go to the gym.

If I can't go to the gym in the morning that means I have to go later when its busy and I hate being there when its busy so I might as well not even go.

When I don't go to the gym it puts me in a pissy mood because the gym is where I get my anger out. To top it all off I got a call from my mom going off on me because she was pissed I wasn't coming home to her house this summer and then the complaining about my dad and asking for money started.

So am I taking my anger out on Jakes sister? Maybe. Do I care? Fuck no she's the reason my day got all fucked up in the first place. I have a routine and she's fucking up that routine.

Ethan tosses an empty water bottle at my head startling me out of my thoughts. "Hey bozo I've been talking to you."

"Fuck off Ethan." I roll my eyes and walk into the kitchen grabbing a water from the fridge.

"I was just asking you if you wanted to just go to the gym later. Geez whats got your panties in a twist?"

"Shut the fuck up no I don't want to go later because it's gonna be crowded." I plop back on the couch twisting open the water bottle.

Ethan just stays silent his eyes focused on the tv. I feel bad for yelling at him but he was pissing me off.

--- Madison Pov ---

I must've fallen asleep I jolted awake to the sound of a loud knock on my door. I jump up and ran to open it.

Jake was standing on the other side. He just stares at me for a second making me nervous but soon breaks out into a big smile and gathers me into a giant bear hug.

"Mads it is so good to see you." "Its good to see you too Jake I missed you." He released me and stepped back he examined me and a frown crossed his face as he leaned closer and examined my eye I flinch away.

"Jake it's not what it looks like." "Then what the fuck is it Madison because it sure as hell looks like fucking black eye." He looks at me expectantly.

"I umm I was super Clumsy and I wasn't watching where I was going and I ran straight into a wall." I laughed it off hoping he would buy it I had always been clumsy growing up so it wouldn't be that hard to buy that I had ran into a wall.

He laughs seeming to have bought it "same old Mads still clumsy." I laugh with him. He smiles and brings me into another hug, "I am really glad you're here I can't wait to hear all about your life in California and catch up." I

stiffen in his arms and step back when he mention's California. "Thanks Jakey I love you too" he looks confused for a second but shrugs it off and pastes a smile on his face.

"Did Nicky already show you where everything was? There's a bathroom right down the hall. In your closet I left a couple clean towels and an extra blanket. There's also extra toothbrushes and stuff in the bathroom cabinets if you need them. Unfortunately theres only one bathroom." He laughed and I laugh with him grateful that talking with him hasn't been as awkward as I was afraid it might be.

It feels like we're jumping right back in from where we left off when he first left. Jake interrupted my thoughts. "Alright let's go eat I believe Noah was cooking tonight." leading me out of the room.

f o u r

J ake and I walked in the kitchen and were greeted by complete chaos. Taylor Swift was blaring and Nicky Jules and Brooke were all scream singing along.

Noah was yelling at Ethan to stop eating the cheese that he was about to put in the quesadillas. Asher was in the corner rolling his eyes.

Nicky grabbed my hand and started dancing with me. Jules and Brooke soon joined in. Brooke grabbed my brothers hand and Jules grabbed Ethan's hand.

We were all jumping around probably looking absolutely nuts. But I was laughing and I was happy for the first time since I can remember.

-Asher's pov-I glanced up from my phone to watch the chaotic dance party that was unfolding in front of me. This was a daily occurrence.

I watched Madison she was laughing and jumping around moving her hips. She was pretty I'll give her that. However it was clear she was used to getting what she wanted.

From what Jake has told me her parents were always doting on her and giving her everything she wanted. Her dad would apparently bring her some sort of gift every time he traveled and thats if the little princess didn't go with him. From what she pulled this morning she clearly hasn't changed.

I liked our friend group I liked the way things were I didn't want things to change I didn't want some spoiled brat coming in and ruining everything.

Jake was also under so much stress and pressure with his job he was working towards getting a promotion.

I don't know why he told Madison she could come now of all times. And why the fuck would she let us know so last minute clearly she doesn't give a fuck about anyone else but herself.

She looks at me and we lock eyes she smiles and then looks away shyly. I roll my eyes and look back down at my phone. A notification popped up Ciara was texting me.

Heyy love we on for tonight?

Yes I'll be there in 10.

I was supposed to meet up with Ciara at some bar I would normally cancel on her but I'm grateful for the excuse to leave. I get up feeling eyes watching me as I head towards the door. and I hear Madison asking if I wasn't staying for dinner.

--- Madison's Pov ---

I watched as Asher got up and left not even saying goodbye to anyone. I asked if he was staying for dinner and Noah shook his head saying "he's probs hanging out with Ciara" I

looked at Jake confused "is Ciara y'all's friend too?" Ethan burst out laughing shaking his head "Absolutely not Ciara is basically Ash's fuck buddy we don't like her."

Jake rolled his eyes "dude chill will the cussing in front of my little sis."
Nicky chimed in "Ciara's just different she just doesn't really make an effort
to be friendly with anyone except ash it's not that we don't like her it's just
that we have never been given the chance to get to know her right Ethan?"
She gave Ethan a pointed look.

Brooke rolled her eyes, "Nicky babe don't sugar coat shit we don't like her
because she's an absolute raging bitch." I laughed at them.

Just then Noah yelled "Quesadillas are done!" Everyone immediately
jumped into action. Nicky was grabbing plates and Jules grabbed a stack
of napkins and Ethan started taking wine glasses out and filling them to
the brim with wine putting one at every spot but with a stern look from
Jake he skipped my spot.

I rolled my eyes. Jake brought a bag of chips and queso to the table and
Noah brought the huge stack of quesadillas.

We all took a seat at the table. I sat in between Jake and Jules. I was surprised
that we were all eating at the table at my house we never ate at the table in
fact it was rare I ate at all to be honest.

My boyfriend thought I needed to lose weight which I mean he was probably right. Everyone started piling things on their plate and passing things
around and everyone was talking and laughing.

I looked at my brother he was laughing at something Brooke had said to
him. He looked so incredibly happy here and I was so happy for him. He
found his family. Plus I totally shipped him and Brooke.

I put a quesadilla on my plate and tried to focus on the conversations
happening around me. Jake and Noah were talking about some football
game. Jules and Nicky were taking about going to the beach this weekend
and what they were gonna wear and Ethan and Brooke were arguing about
who could have the last quesadilla.

I smiled at them I could see myself finding my place here finding my own family just like Jakey. Those nice thoughts were soon interrupted by not so nice thoughts.

I could hear Cades voice in my head screaming at me at how worthless and ugly I was and how no one was ever going to love me and want me because I was disgusting.

I looked down at the quesadilla on my plate half of it was already eaten. You shouldn't have eaten that what is wrong with you you're going to just gain all the weight back you stupid disgusting fat pig. My brain kept telling me over and over again.

I finally stood up keeping the tears at bay. "I'm super tired so I think I'm gonna take a quick shower and head to bed, thank y'all for everything it was amazing to meet you guys." I smiled at them all. "Goodnight Mads we'll see you tomorrow." Jake smiled at me. As I walked off I heard them all say goodnight.

****

TRIGGER WARNING

I ran up the stairs as fast as I could to the bathroom. I turned the shower water on and bent over the toilet.

I shoved 2 fingers down my throat and watched as the half of the quesadilla I ate filled up the toilet. I flushed it and tears flooded my eyes but I wiped them away.

I took off my clothes and got ready to step in the shower. I looked at myself before stepping in. I really was ugly.

Bruises and scars covered my torso and down my legs and arms. I would have to wear long sleeves for a little bit.

Nobody can know how bad it was nobody can know what I've been through. I don't want to risk them seeing me the same way Cade saw me and the way I saw myself.

As soon as I stepped in the shower I collapsed on the floor and just sobbed.

Maybe this was the wrong decision maybe I should go back to Cade it really wasn't all that bad he was only mean when he drank or if he had a bad day.

There would be days where he would be so kind to me and make me feel so loved I miss that Cade the one I fell in love with the one I thought I would spend the rest of my life with.

After showering I ran to my room I forgot my clothes and didn't want anyone to see the bruises. As soon as I got in my bed sleep took over.

f i v e

Asher's Pov -

I stumble into the house at 2 am it seems like everyone was asleep so I make my way up the stairs to my bed. I walk past the guest room and I hear whimpering and crying. I stop for a second outside the door and listen for a second. I want to go in and make sure Madison's okay but I don't know her she doesn't know me it's not my place plus it's probably just a bad dream I shake it off and keep walking to my room. I keep thinking about her though. Maybe I should've gone in. I try and shrug it off and get some sleep. She's just some spoiled brat she's probs having a bad dream that her favorite perfume or some shit is sold out. I laugh to myself and close my eyes.

- Madisons Pov -

TRIGGER WARNING

- nightmare -I'm sobbing my dad is standing over me. "You useless piece of shit. You know after all I've done for you and you still aren't grateful you still fight me. You deserve this. I deserve to have you, you owe me. I get you everything you could ever want and all you had to do was smile and have dinner with me and your mom." He stalks closer to me I cower in the corner sobbing. "Please dad please don't do this I'm so sorry I tried I just miss Jake I'll try harder to smile I'm so sorry." I beg. He laughs "you miss Jake that useless brother of yours you know he clearly didn't give 2 shits about you because he left you here." He steps closer. My body is trembling now. "He didn't know and you know it. You act like everything's fine in front of him and forced me to pretend the bruises are my own clumsiness. He doesn't know what you are like you're a monster and then you and mom drove him a way so he would never find out." He stands there for a second shocked that I would talk back to him. When he registered what I said he grabbed me by the throat and threw me over the couch. He shoved my face down into the cushions and tore my pants. I sobbed and tried to go to a different place but I couldn't I never could. "Please stop you're my dad you're supposed to love me you're not supposed to do that I sob." He slaps me and enters me from behind. I cry harder it hurts so bad. It feels like I'm being ripped apart from the inside.

I wake up sweating and shaking. I take deep breaths trying to calm the panic attack that is brewing inside of me. I feel like the walls are closing in on me I can't breathe. I try and stumble to the door I'm shaking so bad I trip and fall. I finally make it to the door and open it looking around frantically I can't breathe my throat is closing in.

- Asher's Pov -

I hear someone in the hallway. I look over at the time it's 3 am I've only been asleep for an hour. I hear a loud crash. Who the fuck is up at this time making all that noise. I walk out my door preparing to unleash hell on whoever was out there. I look around not seeing anything until my eyes come across her. Madison's on the ground hugging her knees to her chest rocking back and forth gasping for air. It registers in me she's having a panic attack. I quickly run over to her yelling for Jake as I run and kneel down in front of her. "Jake get the fuck out here." I continue to yell. I turn to her. "Madison shh look at me love." She looks me in the eyes her eyes are filled with tears it breaks me heart. "What is 5 things you can see?" I ask her. She looks around just then Jake comes out and is running towards us. "What the fuck happened?" He tries to pull her into his arms but she starts breathing harder and cowers away from him. "Jake hold on man give her some space she's having a panic attack." I turn back to her "Madison tell me what are 5 things you can see?" She looks at me "you, jake, the door, the ceiling, and the floor." I nod at her "good love now tell me what are five things you can feel." I speak to her softly and she grabs my hand. "You, the cold floor, the wall against my back, the air from the vent, and Jake," she grabs jakes hand with her other hand her breathing starts to slow. "Good girl now just take some deep breaths you're okay." She nods her head. Finally her breathing slows to a normal pace and she moves to stand with jakes help. She looks at me "thank you Asher." I nod my head and turn around and walk back to my room. What the hell was that. I shrug it off and try and fall asleep.

- Madison's Pov -Jake looks at my questioningly "are you okay what happened." I nod my head and smile at him trying to show him that everything's okay. "I'm okay jake I'm sorry this was so embarrassing I just had a nightmare I don't know why it turned into a panic attack I don't even remember the nightmare." I lied trying to laugh it off hoping he would buy it. "Okay you don't need to be embarrassed Mads it's no big deal go try and get some sleep okay come get me if you need anything." He spoke softly still looking at me as if he didn't believe a word I was saying. I nodded my head and gave him a hug and walked back into my room. I can't believe I did that. They're going to think I'm crazy. Asher's going to hate me even more now that i woke him up. I berate myself until I eventually fall asleep.

- -

chapter six

I startled awake at the sound of a knock. Jules comes bouncing in. "Hey babe you're finally awake." She smiles. I smile at her. "Umm Goodmorning what's up?" "Well it's technically good afternoon but anyways umm Nicky told me not come in here and bother you but I just wanted to come in and let you know we're all going down to my families beach house this weekend and you're so invited and me and the girls are going shopping today for outfits for it so are you down?" "Oh my god yes I'm so down!" I smiled I'm so excited I can't wait to hangout with them. I don't know the last time I've been able to just go out and have fun with girl friends. Back home when I lived with my parents I wasn't really allowed to do much and Cade never allowed me to go out or anything. "Let me just get dressed real fast." I jump out of bed and start looking through my duffel bag for something somewhat appropriate to go shopping but also something that would cover up my bruises. Jules leaves me to get changed and tells me to meet her out in the living room when I'm ready. I don't have a lot of really cute clothes in my bag because 1 I packed in a hurry and 2 I never really wore anything else except sweats around Cade because anything else would either show off the bruises or cause him to make a comment on my body. I find a cute sweatshirt and a pair of jeans and decide that'll do and throw them on really quickly and slip on my white sneakers.

I then throw my hair up into a claw clip and apply some makeup on my face and I'm ready to go. I head down the stairs and see the whole crew waiting for me in the living room I smile at everyone and hesitantly make my way to the couch to sit next to Jules who is sitting on Ethan's lap. I can feel Asher and Jake staring at me but I avoid looking at them. I lean over to whisper to jules, "are the boys coming with us?" Jules leans over to whisper back but then Ethan leans down and whispers, "what are we whispering about?" I laugh and jules pushes his head away and rolls her eyes and says to me "no they're going to their own stores but they might meet up with us after for dinner." I breathe a sigh of relief I don't think I could handle spending the day with Jake and Asher looking at me all concerned. Nicky and Noah soon join us and we all make our way to different cars. All the girls hop into Nicky's white suv and all the boys hop into Noah's black suv and we wave goodbye. Jules cranks up the radio blaring some 2000's pop music and starts scream singing along I laugh at her. Brooke starts yelling at her to change it and she finally changes it to Taylor swift and we all start singing along. We pull into the parking lot of the mall and make a game plan on which stores we're going to hit up first. We all walk into pacsun upon jules request. I just kind of just tagging along I've never really been able to shop and buy what I like so I have no idea what I'm doing. I do have a lot of money though I was left an inheritance by my dear parents I guess they felt guilty or had nobody else to give it to but I never got around to spending it because I was scared Cade would find out I had it and would take it all. I walked up and down the store and picked up a couple things I thought might look good on me. The girls have arms full of clothing and turn around to see I picked up 2 things a sundress and a long sleeve top. "Girl is that all you're gonna try on I saw that tiny duffel bag you had so I knoww you need clothes?" Jules asks Brooke elbows her "jules." She scolds. "It's okay" I laugh "to be honest I have no idea what I'm doing I've never really shopped for myself before." I said feeling kind of embarrassed to admit it. "Oh my god girl we are going to pop your fucking Cherry we're going to have the best time!" Jules squeals and grabs my arm.

Nicky smiles at me and takes my other arm and says, "we have a couple of rules when it comes to shopping, 1 clothes are meant to fit you not the other way around, 2 find clothes that make you feel good they are for you not for anybody else, and 3 find your color palette which you are 100% a summer meaning we gotta find you bright colors because you're going to look so hot." The girls go through the store picking things out for me and throwing them in the growing pile in my arms. Once my arms are full we all hit the fitting rooms. I try on a couple of sundresses, a few bikinis, some denim shorts, and a few different crop tops that I can mix and match. I love all of it and decide to buy it all the girls have great taste. We hit up a few more stores and I buy a ton more things and then we stop at Victoria secret. We're all giggling and picking hot as fuck lingerie sets for eachother to try on. My arms are full of lacy panty and bra sets and a couple hot lacy body suits and we all head to the fitting rooms I try on the sets and look at myself in the mirror. All I see are bruises and scars I don't even recognize myself anymore I bite back the tears and close my eyes and whisper to myself "the bruises do not define you." I open my eyes and look at myself again still seeing the same thing I groan and a silent tear slips out. I decide to buy all of it just to make the girls happy. I come out of the fitting room with my arms full and start to make my way to the register when I see the other girls talking to the boys. Oh great I say to myself. Me and Asher make eye contact and he looks down at everything I'm holding and then smirks my cheeks immediately turn bright red and I basically run to the register to checkout as fast as I can so we can leave. I hear jake yelling at the girls. "Why the fuck would you bring my little sister here she doesn't need any of this crap." Brook steps right in front of him. "First of all you can stop the yelling try and yell at us again and I'll flatten you in 2 seconds. Second of all your sister is 18 years old she's a big girl she can decide for herself what she does and doesn't need besides she's hot af she needs some hot lingerie to match that bod." Brooke turns around and winks at me and I laugh. Jake just shakes his head but backs down. I clear my throat suddenly feeling awkward that my brother knows I bought lingerie but you know what he can get over it. "Alright well that was hot but I'm hungry so can we go get lunch now." Ethan asked. Jules punches his arm "oww what was that for." "Read the room Ethan."

We all make our way to the food court. The guys immediately head over to the burger stand and me and the girls make a beeline to chick fil a. I order a Cobb salad and a diet lemonade. After we all get our food we find a table and all sit down. After dinner we all head back to the cars to go back home.

chapter seven

As soon as we get home we're all peacefully sitting in the living room watching some reality tv show except for Jules and Ethan they went off by themselves somewhere. when all of the sudden Jules and Ethan burst in squealing holding a box full of what looks like air mattresses. They are literally the same person I swear but I totally ship them. "SLEEPOVER!" they both squeal. Asher, jake and Noah roll their eyes but nicki and Brooke jump up and start squealing with Ethan jules. I laugh at them "I'm so down!"

Pretty soon after only a little convincing from Jules she has Noah, Asher, Jake, and Ethan blowing up the blow up mattresses while us girls are in the kitchen putting charcuterie boards together and making popcorn. After everything's ready we all change into our pajamas

I change into this and bring out my weighted stuffed bunny. It helps with my anxiety and helps me to fall asleep. I also grab my favorite fluffy blanket and slippers and head out to the living room where everyone else has already curled up in their chosen air mattress or on the couch. Brooke is sitting on my brothers lap and is arguing with Ethan on what movie we were gonna watch. They're always arguing about something I laugh to myself and take a seat on the couch between my brother and Asher.

We finally decided on one of the die hard movies I guess Brooke won that argument.

The movie starts and I can feel my eyes getting heavier and heavier. I hadn't really been able to sleep after my nightmare last night. I let sleep take over me and can feel my head resting on a very hard pillow I don't know how that pillow got there and why it's so hard but I'm so tired I don't care so imma just go with it.

- Asher's Pov -

I'm engrossed in the die hard movie when I feel a head drop to my shoulder. I look and see Madison fast asleep. She looks cute when she's asleep. Stop it Asher I berate myself in my head. I shake her off and she jerks awake I know I'm being an asshole but that's what I'm best at. She looks at me confusingly and then when it registers in her mind what happened her cheeks blushed red and she immediately looked to the tv pretending to focus on the movie. I roll my eyes at her and move to get up. I need a cigarette. "I'll be back." I throw over my shoulder as I walk out to the patio. My phone starts ringing and I look at it it's my dad fucking hell what does he want now. I pick up. "Hey dad." "Hey son when the fuck are you coming home?" "Dad I already talked to you about this I'm staying here for the summer." I sighed. "Your mom wants you home." He said getting angrier. "You know why I'm not fucking coming home and so does she and she's not my fucking mom so I really could care less what she wants. Stop fucking calling me about it." I hang up on him I know my words were cruel but he deserved it. I collapse in one of the patio chairs and put my head in my hands. I know they're hurt and they're angry that I chose to stay here this summer. But I had to I couldn't go back there not after what happened. Everything changed after that night they changed and I don't want to fucking see them right now other wise I'm gonna say something or do something I'll regret. I shrug it off and light my cigarette and try and think about something else. My thoughts soon go to Madison. I don't know why I get so pissed off at her she really did nothing to me but the things Jake has told me it breaks my heart for him. I kind of knew how he felt and I never wanted anyone else to feel that way and it makes me angry that Madison helped make him feel that way. Jakes been my best friend since the first day we met at NYU we were both in the same college success class and bonded over the fact our teacher was a complete wack job. I've told him things I haven't told anyone and he's told me things he hasn't told anyone either. For some reason I trust him and I don't usually do that very easily maybe one of the reasons why I'm so pissed that Madison's here is I've gotten so close to all of these people and have become comfortable with them and now some new spoiled rich girl comes in the mix it makes me feel like I have to close myself off again. I hear Jake approaching behind me. "Hey dude you okay?" "Yeah I'm alright just stuff with my dad you know how it is." "Yeah I get it I'm sorry." He reaches his hand out and I hand him a cigarette and we just sit in silence for a minute. "I'm gonna head to bed it's gonna be a long ass day tomorrow." I say and Jake laughs following me inside I laugh with him trying to put up the facade that I'm fine.

chapter eight

I wake up and look around I am the first one awake. The others were still up watching the movie when I passed out. The beach weekend was getting closer. We leave tomorrow and I am getting more and more nervous. I have to figure out how to cover up my bruises before then. I take out my phone and look up and try and find some waterproof body makeup and some better makeup for my face. I find some that I can pickup at Sephora in an hour. I breathe sigh of relief that has been bothering me for days now. Would it be easier to just tell my brother and his friends what I have been through? Probably but I can't I don't want their pity and I don't want to be seen as some weak stupid little girl who didn't have the strength to leave. And most of all I didn't want them to see me how Cade and my dad and I saw me.

Now that I have gotten that figured out I stand up and decide to attempt to make breakfast for everyone I felt like I owed them all tremendously so the least I could do was try and have breakfast ready.

- Ashers Pov -

I startle awake to smoke everywhere and the smoke alarm going off. Everyones waking up and immediately going into action. Noah has the fire extinguisher is trying to distinguish flames coming out of who knows what was in that pan. Jake is running around opening windows and doors. Ethan and Madison are fanning towels in front of the smoke alarm. "What the hell happened." I rush over to help Noah and grabbed the salt and threw it over the flames. "Mads tried cooking breakfast." Noah laughed as the flames finally died down. I look over at Madison who's trying to avoid eye contact at all costs. I laugh what the hell this girl is a complete chaotic tornado you can't leave her alone for a second. I guess perks of being a rich spoiled brat. I roll my eyes. "I'm gonna go take a quick shower."

- Madisons pov -

I feel horrible I have never been good at cooking the first time I cooked for Cade it was a disaster and ended in a particularly rough beating after that he hired our cook Maria but wouldn't let me have whatever she made. Maria was kind though I think if she knew what was happening she would have tried to save food for me but if she had done that I was afraid Cade would get angry at her and do something. So I acted like everything was fine in front of her I was really good at doing that.

I looked around at the chaotic mess I had caused. I was so scared Jake would be mad at me. "Guys I'm so sorry." I look down not making eye contact I learned quickly that eye contact would make Cade even angrier he said I didn't deserve to look him in the eye. I feel arms wrap around me its Nicky. "Babe its okay we have all had this happen in fact Jules was completely banned from the kitchen after her incident of last year." I laugh appreciating her trying to make me feel better. Jake comes around to me too and lifts an arm to playfully punch me in the arm. I flinch but quickly hide it. "Its okay Mads as long as you're okay." "Thanks Jakey." I smile.

Everyone goes their own separate ways and I decide to go take a shower. I look down at my phone to see if my sephora order is ready. I accidentally bump into what I thought was a wall. I grimace as a strong hand grasps my forearm full of bruises trying to steady me. I look up meeting Ashers eyes. "I am so sorry I wasn't watching where I was going." I look down and deeply regret that as soon as I do. I notice he's only wearing a towel and water droplets are dripping down his muscular chest right down to his abs and then his very defined V. I look back up and catch him smirking. "if you are done ogling me now I am trying to get past you love." My face blushed a deep shade of red he's such an asshole I quickly move out of his way and all but run to the bathroom.

Before I get in the shower I decide to call an uber to get me to sephora. I didn't want to bother jake after the chaos I caused this morning. I take a quick shower. When I step out I look into the mirror and examine my bruises its become I daily ritual at this point. I think that maybe if I look at them everyday maybe they'll heal faster its stupid I know but part of me feels that maybe if the bruises heal maybe the memories of how the bruises occured would heal as well. It was always what I hoped after every beating but it never happened the memories stay the scars stay I am scarred inside and out. I am truly ugly. I walk out of the bathroom and run to my room. I change into leggings and a sweatshirt and grab my purse. I look down at my phone and see that my uber has arrived so I run down the stairs and out the door before anyone can see me. I don't want to answer any questions. I see a black SUV pulled up in front of the house so I open the door to the backseat and hop in. "Hello Paul right?" "Yes ma'am." He smiles and stares at me a little too long before turning around and putting the car in drive. I shift uncomfortably in my seat.

About 5 minutes down the road I am lost in my thoughts staring out the window when I feel a hand caressing my ankle. I look down and see that Pauls hand had reached back and its on my ankle and slowly slipping up towards my thigh. I freeze. I look up and see him staring at me through the rearview mirror. I try and shift away but his hand holds me hostage. I begin to panic. This cannot happen right now I just need to get to Sephora.

I pray that we get there soon. My hands are shaking I don't know what to do. I am afraid to say anything that would piss him off and he end up kidnapping me or dropping me off on the side of the road. It feels like I am frozen in place forced to feel something and put up with something that I don't want to again.

Finally we pull into the parking lot of sephora and he removes his hand from my leg. I quickly get my seatbelt off and go to open the door but he beats me to it. As I step out of the car he steps uncomfortably close to me and his hand reaches out to touch my hair and bring it to his nose I quickly try and move past him but just as I walk past him I feel a hand run down my back to my ass and squeeze. I run into Sephora my legs shaking. I try and keep the tears at bay and get myself under control as I walk over to a cashier. I smile at her and tell her my name and she gives me my pickup order. I walk out the doors and sit on the bench pondering how I am going to get home I am terrified of calling another uber. I used to take ubers all the time back home and that never happened but now I am scarred for life. I hesitantly decide to call Jake my hands and legs still shaking. He picks up on the first ring. "Mads where are you the girls were blowing up my phone they were looking for you" "I'm so sorry I am at Sephora right now I took an uber here and something happened and I am scared to call another one I am so sorry Jake can you come pick me up?" I am crying now. "Mads slow down okay deep breaths I am all the way across town but I am going to get someone there to pick you up okay its gonna be okay." "Thanks jakey I love you." "I love you too Mads and we'll talk about this uber driver when I get home im gonna kill them." "Its okay Jake it wasn't that big of a deal I am probably over reacting." "You are not over reacting you're crying and clearly shaking by the sound of your voice but its gonna be okay I am gonna call Asher I think he's at the gym which is near you so just sit tight." Before I can protest he hangs up.

chapter nine

Ashers Pov -

Sweats dripping down my face and I'm taking all my anger out on the punching bag in front of me when I hear my phone ring I look down at my phone and see Jakes calling. He can wait I think to myself and continue punching the fuck out of the punching bag. But after the third time he tries calling me I finally pick up. "Jake what the fuck do you want?" "Geez what crawled up your ass?" "Just tell me what you want." I roll my eyes at him Jake has this extraordinary talent of pushing just the right buttons to piss you off even more when you're already in a bad mood. "I need you to go pick up Madison she is at Sephora down the road from your gym she had an incident with an uber driver and she's freaked out about it." "What the fuck do you mean by incident what the hell happened?" I am already walking towards the locker room to grab my stuff. "I'm not sure I didn't want to ask and waste time I need someone over there as soon as possible she was crying and sounded really shaken up about it." "Alright dude don't worry about it I'll take care of it I am grabbing my stuff and leaving right now."

What the hell did Madison get herself into now I think to myself. I am so pissed off she would put herself in this situation and I am pissed that Jake hadn't told her about the uber drivers here in New York. All the girls know not to take a fucking uber to either drive themselves or ask any of us to drive them. The uber drivers here are sketchy as fuck what was she thinking. I race to my car and speed to sephora and may or may not have ran a few red lights.

When I pull up in front of Sephora I see Madison sitting on a bench hugging her knees to her chest. I park right in front of the store not giving a shit if someone gets pissed off. I get out and walk over to her. "Madison come on I'm taking you home." She looks up and tears stain her face my heart breaks seeing her like that. Why the fuck is she affecting me this way its pissing me off. I walk away and open her door and motion for her to get in. She gets in and smiles her thanks at me I just nod my head. I walk around to the other side and take a deep breath before I get in preparing to give her a lecture.

"Madison what the fuck is wrong with you what were you thinking?" She looks at me startled and doesn't say a word so I continue. "What did he do?" She shakes her head and looks down at her lap. I grasp her chin and force her to look at me and I say more sternly "Madison what did he do? We're not leaving until you tell me what he did and what his name is?" "Why do you care?" She says defiance in her eyes. "You are Jakes baby sister and hes been like a brother to me thats why now fucking answer the question." A tear drips down her face. "He reached his hand back and umm." She pauses. "and...?" I ask expectantly. "He put his hand on my ankle and he umm he umm he was..." She pauses again. "This is stupid I am just overreacting I am being stupid it really wasn't that big of a deal." She rambles. "Finish." I say firmly. "He brushed his hand up and down my leg and touching my thigh and then when I got out he grabbed my hair and sniffed it and then he brushed his hand down my back and squeezed my butt." Her cheeks blush red and she shakes her head out of my hold and looks back down at her lap. I lean back in my seat and sigh I am gonna have to kill this motherfucker what the hell is wrong with people. "What was his name?" "Paul." She whispered softly. "Please don't do anything it really isn't that big of a deal it was my own fault really I mean my ex warned me not to wear leggings out that it just meant I was asking for it I should have known better." She rambles. "Stop." I look at her astonishingly this girl just got asualted by a fucking uber driver and shes blaming herself. "This is not your fault that man should have known to keep his fucking hands to himself and since he does not he will have to deal with consequences I will call when we get home and get his ass fired. From now on... Madison look at me." She looks up at me. "You will not take an uber again ask any one of us and we will give you a ride fuck theres a million people in that house that could have driven you theres no reason to get in the car with some rando that was irresponsible you need to be more careful this is not California where you get to go off and do whatever the fuck you want off of daddy and rich boyfriends money." "I'm sorry you had to come get me but you don't have to act like an ass." she bites back. "I didn't want to bother anyone." "Thats bullshit because you clearly didn't care about bothering anyone when you told us so last minute that you were coming. You don't get to just do whatever you please welcome to reality love." "You don't fucking know anything about my life and you don't know me you dick so fuck off." She turns away and I hear her sniffle. Fuck now I feel bad. I turn up the music drowning out sniffles and ignore her the rest of the ride back to the house. I am so pissed at her that she would be so careless with her safety.

chapter ten

I wake up to the sound of my alarm its 7 am we leave for Jules beach house at 8. I hop out of bed and go to the bathroom to brush my teeth and take a quick shower. As soon as I step in the shower it sometimes feels like all my worries wash down the drain with the water. Showers became my escape. The only time I got to focus on myself. However this time when I stepped in the shower it seemed like I only became more anxious. I have been stressed out about going on this beach trip because I am terrified they will figure out my secret. I am terrified the makeup will wash off and reveal my broken and used body. That can't happen. Beach trips with friends are supposed to be fun but because of Cade I dread every part of this trip and that makes me hate him but the sick truth is I feel like part of me still loves him and wants to protect him. And the sickest truth of all I think I miss him. I unblocked his number last night. I couldn't sleep I was restless so I looked through our old messages the one that used to make me smile so hard the ones that used to make my cheeks blush red. I shrug off the thoughts and focus on washing my hair the girls had made me buy some vanilla scented body wash and shampoo and conditioner. Call me basic but I love the vanilla scent in some ways it makes me feel safe.

I step out of the shower and debate blow drying and straightening my hair I decide against it it'll only get wet when we hit the beach. I swallow back another wave of anxiety and head to my room to change. I lock the door and examine my naked body in the mirror I hate the sight of it. I quickly get to work and pull out the body makeup I had bought the other day and spread it all over my body praying it will cover the bruises. It did thank god. I take one more look at my body in the mirror and once I decide I'm satisfied I change into some jean shorts and crop top and throw on white button up as a precaution for the bruises on my arms. I throw some makeup on my face and throw my hair up into a claw clip add some jewelry and I am finally ready. I grab a couple outfits and essentials that I'll need and throw it all into my duffel bag and make my way to the stairs. As I walk out of my room Noah and Nicky are walking out of theres. Nicky smiles at me "Good morning babe how did you sleep?" I smiled at her "Good morning I slept good that bed in there is so freaking comfy." she laughs and Noah approaches me and grabs my bag from me. "Oh you seriously don't have to do that." "Its no worries at all our girls don't carry bags down the stairs if our hands our free and Nicky and I's bags are already downstairs." I smile at him shyly. "Thank you." He smiles back and motions for me and Nicky to go ahead of him down the stairs. Noah seems really kind he kind of seems like an old man at heart he doesn't say much but he has this way that he carries himself that makes him seem mature and wise. Him and Nicky are for sure the parents of the group. I smile to myself

^^^ Madisons Outfit ^^^

We walk into the living room and everyones on the couch waiting for us. "AHH you look so good like damnnn girl!" Jules jumps up and gives me a hug. I laugh "Thanks Jules so do you I love that color on you." Noah comes back in from putting the bag in the car. "Alright are we ready to go?" Everyone jumps up and starts making it to the door. "We have about an hour long car ride and 8 of us so we're gonna split into 2 cars so that its more comfortable and it'll be good to have 2 cars when we get there. So we'll have Jake, Asher, Brooke, and Mads, in one and Jules, Ethan, and Nicky, y'all will be with me." Everyone nods their heads and makes their way to their assigned car not questioning Noah. I hate that I have to ride in the same car as Asher after him yelling at me yesterday for no damn reason I refuse to make eye contact with him or talk to him. He doesn't know anything about my life. However I am excited to get to know Brooke better hopefully. She seems kind of closed off and hard to get a read on and I haven't been able to talk to her that much.

Asher gets in the drivers seat and my brother gets in the passenger seat leaving the backseat for me and Brooke. Asher starts the car and some rap music I don't know if you can even really call it music blares through the speakers. Jake immediately starts rapping along and Asher joins in. Brooke leans forward and grabs Ashers phone and turns the volume down. "If me and Mads are gonna be stuck in this car with you two bozos for an hour you better believe we're choosing the music." Jake turns around to argue with her but she glares at him and hands me the phone and he quickly turns back around. Asher flips her off but doesn't argue. I click on the search button and search up the sophia the first theme song. I know every word but only because I watched it with the kids I would babysit which I definitely did not force them to watch it. I tell Jake to crank up the volume and I press play. The song comes blaring through the speakers and I see Asher roll his eyes. Brooke looks at me and squeals "OMG I love this song." We both scream sing along and Jake and Asher just look at us like we're completely nuts.

About 15 minutes in Jake gets a call from Nicky and puts it on speaker. "Hey Nicky you're on speaker whats up?" "So Ethan has informed us he has to pee really bad so theres a gas station up ahead so we're stopping there." Asher rolls his eyes "Are you serious already it's only been 15 minutes? He does this every time." "I told him to go before we left but he didn't listen."

Noah chimes in. "I didn't have to go then." Ethan whines. I hear Jules and Nicky laughing in the background. "Alright well I guess we'll follow you but tell Ethan this is the last time. He's cut off from all liquids." Jake says into the phone before hanging up. We see a busy bee up ahead and follow Noahs car into the parking lot. "Fuck yeah I love busy bees they have the have the nicest bathrooms and great snacks." Brooke exclaims. We all get out of the car and I follow the girls into the bathroom. "Oooh this is a great opportunity for a mirror pic everyone get in!" Jules runs to the mirror excitedly. We all smile and she takes a few. "We are so hot omg." Brooke says.

After we all peed and Brooke picked out a couple snacks and I grab a water we all get back in the car and get back on the road.

chapter eleven

After what seems like forever we finally pull into the drive way of the beach house its so cute and looks to be on its own private beach. Theres already a car waiting in the driveway and a blonde girl hops out and waves at us excitedly. "Fucking Ciara what the fuck is she doing her Asher?" Brooke exclaims. "She wanted to come Jules said it was fine what do you care." Brooke just rolls her eyes. "You are an asshole you know that right." Asher just shrugs his shoulders and smiles at her which seems to just piss her off even more. When we all get out Ciara runs to Asher and wraps her arms around him. "Hey guys." She turns to look at us and smiles. Brooke just walks straight past her and follows Jules inside. I smile at her and say hi and move past her to follow the girls. "Who the fuck is that bimbo?" I hear her ask Asher. I hurry up and get inside I don't want to hear Ashers response.

--- Ashers Pov ---

"Shut the fuck up Ciara don't talk about her that way thats my best friend's little sister." I brush past her and go to help Jake with the bags. She's so annoying I don't even know why I invited her but she begged to come when I mentioned it. I should've just told her no but she had promised to be nice to the other girls. "You okay?" Jake asks me. "Yeah why?" "You just had zoned out dude I have been holding this bag out for you to take for ages now." I punch him in his arm and roll my eyes. I grab the bag and he laughs following me inside. Jules was giving out room assignments. "Okay so we don't have a lot of rooms because it's usually just me and my sister and my parents so theres only 4 bedrooms and the couch. So let's do Nicky and Noah, Ethan and Jake, Me, Brooke, and Madison, and then I guess Asher and Ciara." Everyone grabs their bags and goes to their assigned rooms. I roll my eyes as Ciara squeals excitedly that we're rooming together. "After everyone gets settled we're going to the beach so y'all better hurry the fuck up." Ethan shouts over his shoulder as he runs down the hall. I set mine and Ciara's bags down and dig through my bag to find my swim trunks and then go to the bathroom to change.

--- Madisons Pov ---

I grab my green bikini and my body makeup from my bag and go into the bathroom to change. I put the bikini on and put a little more makeup on spots that it rubbed off and then put on my white button up over it. I walk down to the living room with Brooke and Jules and everyones in the living room ready to go. Ciara looks me up and down snickers and makes a face of disgust. I look down at my body hoping that I didn't miss a bruise I didn't see anything I look up and she was whispering into Ashers ear. I try and shake it off and not take it too personally but it doesn't work now I'm insecure thanks Ciara.

After we're all ready we all walk down to the beach its beautiful. The girls and I set out a blanket and lay down and the boys bring out a football and start playing. I have a book in front of me but instead I'm watching the boys play and am entirely engrossed in it. Asher took off his shirt and I'm trying not to stare too long but god he's hot. I watch as he tackles Ethan to the ground easily his muscles flexing as he does. I feel someone tap my shoulder I turn and see Ciara sitting next to me smiling but its not a genuine smile its the kind of fake condescending smile. "He's hot isn't he." She says. "I didn't notice." I look back down at my book trying to ignore her. "You know we're dating right?" I ignore her. "Besides you know that he would never go for someone like you." She looks down at my body in disgust. "You know I am just trying to be a good friend and I am completely honest with my friends you might want to start going to gym it might help tone you out a little bit." She laughs. "Thanks for your advice but I'm not interested in Asher." I smile at her trying to not let her hurtful words get to me. I look back at my book. "You know what Ciara why don't you fuck off and leave Madison alone nobody asked for your advice and Madison is absolutely stunning so for the love of god leave her the fuck alone because I will not hesitate to punch a bitch." Brooke says from her spot next to me glaring at her. Ciara looks at her and smiles her condescending smile. "You know Brooke you might wanna take some of my advice." Brooke smiles in a way that makes me scared of her. "Ciara babe if I took your advice I would look like you and in that case all I would be is somebody's miserable lonely depressed fuck buddy instead of having a boyfriend that treats me with respect and love so respectfully you can stop reflecting your own insecurities on me and Madison." She stands up and motions for me to stand with her and we walk to the bathroom. I can feel the tears streaming down my face as I follow her. She opens the door for me and sees my face. "Oh babe please don't take anything she says to heart she's just reflecting she's so insecure with herself that she has to make others feel bad in order to make herself feel better just ignore her." She hugs me. "Thanks Brooke that means a lot to me and thank you for defending me." "Anytime Mads no go wipe your face Im gonna piss and then we're going to go back out there looking hot as ever." I smile at her and wipe the tears off my face some of the makeup comes off my black eye but I don't mind that as much Jake had already seen that and had bought the excuse some of the others might question it though. Brooke comes out of the bathroom and washes her hands and goes to open the door but she looks at my face closer. "What happened to your eye?" "Oh I am super clumsy and I wasn't watching where I was going and walked right smack into a wall." I laughed she laughed with me but still looked at me weirdly as if she didn't buy it but thankfully didn't ask anymore questions. We go back and join the others.

After hanging out at the beach for a little bit we all go back to the house and get ready to eat dinner.

chapter twelve

I look over at the clock its 2 am but I can't sleep. I look over and see Jules and Brooke sound asleep both snoring. I decide to sneak out of the room and go for a night swim in the pool by myself. I throw on a bikini and put a little of the body makeup on but not too much I don't think I'll see anyone. I put an oversized t shirt on that I had stolen from Cade and make my way out to the back deck. I look around and when I don't see anyone I take my shirt off and slowly step in. It feels amazing I close my eyes and just float in the water for a second I hear a deep voice startle me out of my thoughts. "What are you doing?" I look up and see Asher sitting at the edge of the pool staring at me. I roll my eyes at him. "What does it look like I'm doing." I swim away from him. He gets in the pool and strips his t shirt off and swims closer to me his muscles flexing as he does. "Why?" He asks staring into my eyes. I shift uncomfortably and look away eye contact makes me uncomfortable. "I couldn't sleep." I shrug my shoulders and lean my elbows onto the pool wall and rest my head. "Me either Ciaras snoring so loud." I laugh at that. "Brooke told me what she said to you." He whispers almost afraid to bring it up. "Its whatever it doesn't matter." I look the opposite direction from him not wanting him to see how much it bothered me. "It does you didn't deserve that. She's leaving tomorrow morning I called an Uber for her." "You didn't have to do that." "I don't want her here and the girls don't either." "If you didn't want her here why did you invite her." I turn to look at him. "For a distraction I guess." He shrugs his shoulder. "A distraction from what?" I prod. "It doesn't matter." He laughs it off but I can see theres pain behind his eyes. "It does matter everyone deserves to be heard and I am here if you need someone to talk to." He seems uncomfortable but smiles and nods at me. "I'm sorry for being such an ass the other day when I picked you up." I smile and shrug "Its alright." "You scared the shit out of me it could've been much worst." "I know I've seen worst." I say before thinking. He looks at me and his eyes fill with anger. "What did you say?" "Nothing forget I said that I don't know why I said it. I go to look away but he grabs my chin and forces me to look at him. "What do you mean by you've seen worst." "Nothing." I say. He lets me go and I get out of the water I feel his eyes on the back of my thighs I look down at my legs and see some of the makeup had wiped off fuck I quickly throw my t shirt over my head so he won't see the ones on my stomach those are much worst. "What is that?" He gets out and asks me clenching his fists. "Whats what." I ask innocently. He comes closer to me and sits me down on one of the patio chairs your thigh why is there a huge bruise there. He takes my leg in his hand examining my leg. I shiver at the feeling of his hands on my leg. I think he notices my shiver because he chuckles but quickly tries to hide it with a cough. His hands on my leg shouldn't feel this good but they do. His hand starts traveling farther up my thigh and I find myself wanting it to travel up just a little bit higher. His hand stops at a spot on the inside of my thigh examining a bruise there. I swallow back a moan. Stop it Madison I berate myself I try and yank my leg out of his grip but he doesn't let me. "Its nothing I'm super clumsy and fell down some stairs back in California nothing to worry about." I smile at him he doesn't seem convinced but he lets me go.

--- Ashers Pov ---

I watch as she leaves. He leg was covered in bruises I don't buy her falling down stairs. Not to mention the black eye she had but told everyone was because she ran into a wall. I am no expert but I do know it would be very hard to get a black eye simply by running into a wall so I know thats bullshit. Jake told me she was super clumsy growing up and that it was just typical Madison when I had questioned him about it. I try and shrug it off and am hoping that Jakes right that she's just super clumsy but I can't shake the feeling that something is wrong. I get out of the pool and dry off. I decide to crash on the couch not wanting to listen to Ciara's snores. When Brooke told me what Ciara said I was so pissed off. She cried when I told her she was leaving tomorrow but I wasn't gonna buy that shit. Nobody gets to come in here and treat my friends like shit. She won't be coming around again. I try and get some sleep but I can't stop thinking about Madison. The way her thigh felt in my hand and the way she shivered when I touched her she was so beautiful my cock grows hard fuck. I get in and take a very cold shower I can't be thinking about her this way She's Jakes baby sister for god sake. As much as I tell myself that I can't stop thinking about what her mouth would feel around me as I stroke myself in the shower. I groan as I come. I shower quickly and then get out and try and get some sleep before everyone gets up. Ciara's uber is supposed to be here by 7 I wanted her out of here as soon as possible.

--- Authors Note ---

AHH I just wrote my first somewhat spicy scene its way harder than you'd think lmao. I am so sorry if its cringey but I'm easing myself into it so bear with me and please share your opinions with me lmaoo! There will definitely be more to come. ;)

chapter thirteen

P ossible ED trigger warning

--- Madisons Pov ---

I wake up it looks like Jules and Brooke had already gotten up. I look in the mirror my hair is a wreck.

I couldn't stop tossing and turning last night. I couldn't stop thinking about my interaction with Asher.

Why would he care? He has hated me from the day I arrived and never tried to hide the fact.

I throw it up in a messy bun. I hear laughter coming from downstairs so I follow it into the kitchen.

Nicky, Brooke, and Jules are all sitting around the kitchen island drinking their coffee. Jakes at the stove cooking eggs. "Good morning I will say you look absolutely angelic in the mornings." Jake looks at me laughing. I flip him off. I have never been a morning person.

"You want some coffee?" Nicky asks me moving to get up to fix me some.

"I would love some thank you." I smile at her.

I love Nicky she's the most genuine and kind person that I have ever met.

I watch as she grabs a mug out and pours some in. She hands it to me. "Theres cream in the fridge and sugar on the counter if you need it."

"Thanks Nicky." I take a seat next to Jules. I drink my coffee black less calories that way. Cade never let me have it any other way so I guess I just got used to it.

"Who wants eggs?" Jake spoke up.

Everyone raises their hand except me. Jake looks at me pointedly. "You want some?"

"I'm okay, I'm not a big breakfast person." I lie.

He looks at me for a second as if not believing me. but then just nods his head and focuses on filling up the plates with eggs.

Ethan comes running in followed by Noah and then Asher. Ciara must be gone already I think to myself. Asher makes eye contact with me but I quickly look away. "I smelled eggs." Ethan says dramatically sniffing the air.

Jake slaps him on the back of the head and hands him a plate. Ethan's eyes light up and he immediately digs in. I laugh at him.

Everyone has a plate and is eating either at the island or in the breakfast nook. "Why aren't you eating?" Asher suddenly asks looking at me.

"I'm not a breakfast person." I say trying not to make eye contact. "Hm." Is all he says still staring at me. I shift uncomfortably.

"Well anyways I was thinking we could go the lake today and go see the waterfall since we went to the beach yesterday." Jules says trying to change the subject.

"Yes I've dying to go I want to jump off the cliff again." Ethan says. "Alright then It's settled how about we all try and be ready to go by 10?" Noah said looking around. Nobody argues with him.

After breakfast everyone goes to get ready. I look through my bag and grab one of my bikinis, a pair of shorts and a sweatshirt. I grab my body makeup too and go to the bathroom.

I quickly spread the makeup on and change its already 9:45. I my hair is naturally wavy so I decide to leave it natural and do 2 small braids in the front of my hair and call it a day.

^^^The fit ^^^

After everyones ready. We all decide to try and pile into one car. Ethans driving. Noahs in the passenger seat and Nickys on his lap. Brook is on Jakes lap, I'm in the middle on Jules lap, and Ashers next to me.

I don't know who let Ethan drive he's an awful driver. He hits a bump in the road and Jules try to hold onto me but I almost lurch forward. Ashers arm reaches out and catches me. "Ethan what the fuck." Jake yells out.

"Sorry guys my bad." Ethan says sheepishly.

"Jules let Mads sit on Ashers lap. I love you but I don't trust Ethans driving." Jake said glaring at Ethan.

"Me either." Jules says punching Ethan lightly in the arm. "Okay y'all I said I'm sorry it's my bad." Ethan throws his hands up in surrender. "Ethan for the love of god keep both hands on the wheel!" Noah yells. "Sorry, sorry."

Ethan quickly puts his hands back on the wheel. I look at Asher he just nods his head and opens his arms for me.

"Jake really I'm okay." "Stop arguing and come here theres gonna be more bumps in the road." Asher grabs my arm and pulls me onto his lap. I mutter a thanks and try and focus on anything else except for the fact that I'm on his lap.

We finally pull into a parking lot and all pile out. We all follow Jules as she leads us down a path to secluded part of the lake.

^^^The lake^^^

I stop and just stare at it its breathtaking I've never seen anything like it. "Its beautiful isn't it?" Jake says from beside me. I nod my head in awe. Growing up Jake and I never really got to go on any vacations or see anything we were always left with the nanny. Honestly how we grew up felt like we were in prison.

"Come on let's go." Jules laughs and strips off her shorts. Everyone else quickly follows her lead and we all run into the water.

I swim a little ways away from the group and go through the waterfall. Theres a cave behind the waterfall. I swim a little farther into the cave

^^^ Heres kind of what I imagined the cave to look like ^^^

I hear someone following me. I turn around and see Asher following me. I roll my eyes and ignore him and continue swimming deeper into the cave.

"Where are you going?" Asher asks. "None of your business quit following me." I swim faster but he easily matches my pace. "What do you want Asher?"

"I want to continue our conversation from yesterday. I don't buy your story about the bruises Madison its bullshit." He says trying to catch my eyes but I look away from him.

He swims closer to me and forces me to face him. "Talk to me Madison what is going on."

I can't tell him no one can know. "Why the fuck do you care I just want you to leave me alone Asher!" I shout at him. "No!" He shouts back. "I don't give a shit what you want Madison I'm not leaving you alone until you tell me how the fuck you got those..." I crash my lips into his just trying to shut him up.

He jerks back. "What the fuck was that?" "I'm sorry I..." He crashes his lips into mine and takes control. He pulls my body flush against his. His hands come to my thighs and he pulls me up. I wrap my legs around his waist.

I moan against his mouth when his hands travel down squeezing my ass. He kisses me deeper and shoves his tongue in my mouth. Our tongues fight for control but he wins. His hands travel up and palms my breast his thumb swipes at my nipple. Another moan escapes me "Asher."

That seems to wake him up he jumps back. "Fuck." He mutters to himself. I look at him. "Why did you stop." I ask out of breath.

Before he can answer we hear Jules calling our names its time to head back.

The car ride back was uncomfortable to say the least.

--- IMPORTANT Authors Note (Please Read) ---

Hey loves I hope y'all enjoyed this chapter I really had a lot of fun writing this one. I just wanted to give a quick shout out DawnxxDaisy for her good advice on making paragraphs shorter so that readers can comment on different parts of the story. Definitely go check out her stories. At some point soon I will go back and fix the other chapters to make the paragraphs shorter and so I apologize in advance if y'all get a ton of notifications about that lol. But for now I will be leaving on a trip tomorrow and will be gone for a week. With that being said I'm not sure if I'll have time to write so I'm going to try and get out a few chapters today to hold y'all over! Thank you all for all of your support it means a lot!

chapter fourteen

Everyone was asleep and I was not yet again. I was exhausted but I was terrified of having another nightmare. I got out of bed, grabbed a bikini and my makeup, and changed sneaking past Jules and Brooke so I don't wake them.

I go downstairs and out the back door hoping Ashers is not awake this time but secretly hoping he comes out. Don't get me wrong he's such an asshole but when it is just me and him. He's different less closed off.

I step into the pool and immediately feel my body relax. It feels like I'm always tensed up waiting for the other shoe to drop, but when I feel the water hit my skin it is like all my problems wash away hence, the reason showers were my escape when I lived with Cade and my parents.

I hear the back door open and close and someone sits down at the edge of the pool. I know who it is I can smell the cigarette smoke.

"You gonna acknowledge I'm here love or are you gonna ignore me? Don't get shy on me now." Asher says laughing. I turn around and face him. "I'm debating. Sometimes if you ignore things they go away." I say shrugging my shoulders. "Touche." He laughs.

"You know cigarettes are bad for you." I say swimming closer. "No really? thats news to me." He says sarcastically. I roll my eyes at him. We just stare at each other for a second.

He breaks the silence. "What are the bruises from Madison." I shake my head. "Oh my god you just never stop do you?" I laugh. "Don't avoid the question." "I'm not avoiding the question. I've already answered your question multiple times. I've told you where they are from so stop asking." I swim away from him.

He strips off his shirt and extinguishes the cigarette. He jumps in and I swim faster he easily catches up to me. He grabs my arms and pulls me to face him. "I don't believe you but I am here when you are ready to talk about it. A wise person once told me that everyone deserves to be heard." I smile. "Thank you Asher."

He leans in closer and brushes his lips against mine. His lips feel warm and soft against mine like they belong there. I open my lips inviting him in. His tongue laps gently against mine. His hand dives under my bikini top and pinches my nipple. My nipple hardens at the contact. He groans "You drive me crazy." He pulls me flush against his chest I wrap my legs around him and he pushes me against the pool wall. He pushes his hips against mine and I feel his erection against my core. I moan.

I buck my hips against him. "You better stop doing that unless you want me to take your bottoms off right here and fuck you against the wall." He whispers into my mouth. I shiver at his words. His lips leave mine and he tugs on my lower lip with his teeth before trailing his lips down the side of my neck. I moan "Asher please."

"What do you need love?" He asks looking into my eyes. "I need you." He smiles. "I know love but not tonight." I whimper I look at him confused. He kisses my lips again before putting me down. "You don't know me

Madison you don't even know if this is what you want." He says pulling me with him to get out of the pool.

We both dry off and he sits down on a lounge chair and pulls me to lay on his chest facing him. "I want to know everything about you." He says looking at me. I nod my head. "How about 20 questions?" I ask. He laughs but nods his head. "Okay you go first."

"Whats your favorite color" I ask. "Blue." He says. "Eh basic." I say laughing. "Hmm okay whats yours then." 'Pink." I smile sheepishly. "That's just as basic." He argues.

"Alright, alright, whats your favorite drink?" "Whiskey whats yours." "Straight Vodka." I say not even hesitating. He laughs.

We talk for hours about anything and everything. I feel myself dozing off but I keep trying to shake myself awake. I'm terrified of falling asleep.

"You can sleep love." Asher whispers as he strokes my hair. "I can't." I shake my head. "The nightmares?" He questions. I nod. "I'll be here, you're safe you can sleep." I nod against his chest and allow sleep to take over.

TRIGGER WARNING

— Nightmare —

"Stop please, please stop." I whimper. "Shut the fuck up whore." Cade yanks my hair back. He's inside me and holding me down. I'm trapped. It hurts so bad i just want it all to end. Pain shoots up and down my leg as he thrusts in and out.

I try and close my eyes and imagine I'm somewhere else but the pain keeps bringing me back. It always does. His hands are gripping my hips. I know I'll be bruised tomorrow. He's grunting against me. "You are worthless you know that? I am the only person who will tolerate you nobody else wants you. Not even your own parents loved you."

"Your own dad raped you and you know why? Because you are a disgusting whore thats all you are and all you ever will be."

I had opened up to him about my parents when I first fell in love with him. Back when I didn't know the type of person that he was.

Since then I've learned its better to stay quiet and not open up to people because it only ends in getting hurt.

I bite back the tears he won't see me fall apart I won't let him because that is what he wants. He craves the feeling that he gets when he tears people down enough to where they crumble because then he is able to control them. They are left completely defenseless.

I startle awake panting and sobbing. I'm not in the room with the girls where am I. My breathing gets heavier my throat starts closing in I know whats about to happen. I can't breathe.

I feel someone grab my hands. I meet Asher's eyes. "Its okay Madison I'm here. Breathe you're okay. You're safe." My breathing calms.

Asher pulls me into his arms and I just cry and he lets me. "Its okay love let it out. You're safe now." He strokes my hair soothingly. Eventually I fall back asleep to his voice. I feel safe with him.

chapter fifteen

-- TRIGGER WARNING (This is going to be a heavy chapter that will
deal with self-harm as well as the main character will experience what it
feels like to be in a trauma bond so please do not read if you think you will
be triggered.)

All the girls and I are getting ready. There's a bonfire going on at the beach
tonight and we decided to go as a good way to end our last night.

Asher's been avoiding me all day. I don't really know why. When I woke up
this morning he was gone. Maybe I'm just overthinking it but I can't get
the thought that he's avoiding me out of my head.

I've mostly stayed in bed I haven't really been in the mood to do anything
today. I really didn't want to go to this party but Jules begged me to so I
caved. I would do anything to make that girl happy I swear she reminds me
of a golden retriever puppy and I love it. Plus she did say there would be
alcohol there so that made me feel better.

"Mads!" I look up to see Brooke, Nicky, and Jules staring at me. "Are you
okay? We've been talking to you."

"Yes, I'm sorry I must've zoned out." I paste a smile on my face. "Whats up?"

"We were just trying to figure out what to wear." Jules laughed and held up 2 skirt options in front of her definitely the Pink one I tell her.

I look down to see my phone lighting up Cades calling me. Ever since I unblocked him he's been calling me every day without fail but I haven't been able to bring myself to block him again.

"Guys I'll be right back." I run into the bathroom and answer. "Hello."

"Oh so now you'll answer the phone. I've been calling you." "You have to stop calling Cade please stop calling. Please just leave me alone." "Why did you leave me and what we had? You know if you come back I won't hold it against you. I would forgive you."

"I... I'm not coming back Cade." My voice breaks. "Why? You clearly miss me. I was only blocked for two days."

"I should never have unblocked you I'm sorry." "You gave me false hope you realize that right? That was cruel."

"I'm so sorry Cade I know that." "Its okay I forgive you. I guess I'm just disappointed in your behavior you're better than this. Your parents would be so disappointed. It's only a matter of time before Jake finds out what kind of person you are and kicks you out. I'm the only person that truly cares about you Madison."

I pause for a minute not knowing what to say he just confirmed all of my fears. "Cade..." I start but he interrupts me. "Jake doesn't care about you the way I do. He doesn't even know you the way I do."

I panic and hangup the phone. I try and swallow back the tears. What is wrong with me. Maybe he's right maybe he really is the only person that cares about me and thats why I can't bring myself to block him.

He's the only one that would actually put up with all my shit. I'm not a good person. I'm not an easy person to love and Jake and everyone hasn't seen that part of me yet. The broken high maintenance part. I mean Asher saw only a little tiny part of it and it seems to me he is already ready to leave.

I look around not realizing what I'm looking for until I see it. My eyebrow razor. I pick it up and crumble to the floor. I rock back and forth and try and convince myself not to use it that it won't make me feel better but my thoughts are too much I just want to be distracted for just a second. I'll just allow myself to do it this one time.

I pull my pants down and drag the razor across my thigh. I watch as blood drips from the cut it stings. I'm crying harder now it hurts so bad but my thoughts of what Cade has said has stopped and now I only am thinking of the physical pain.

I draw the razor across my thigh one more time below the other cut. I hear a knock at the door its Nicky. "Mads are you okay?" "Yeah just one second." I yell out.

I blot the cuts with toilet paper and wince as I pull my pants up and they brush against the cuts. I take a deep breath and put a smile on my face before walking out.

Nicky looks up looking concerned. "Mads are you okay? You've been acting off today?" "Yes I'm so good I'm sorry I think something just didn't settle well in my stomach but I'm good now. Let's go finish getting ready for the bonfire" I smile at her and she seems to buy it.

I put on some minimal makeup and curl my hair. We all decided to kind of match and wear tube tops and different skirts so I grab my outfit and change in the bathroom.

^^^ The Fit ^^^

After everyones ready we all walk down to the beach. When we get there the beach is packed. Theres a bonfire in the middle and a table set up lined up with alcohol and music blaring. Most of the people there already seem to be drunk. I immediately head to the table and pour myself a shot. I down it and grab a beer.

Asher comes up behind me. "You've been avoiding me." I say. "Of course not I've just been busy today thats all." "Hmm." Is all I say before walking away.

Out of nowhere Jules comes and grabs my arm dragging me to where Nicky and Brooke is dancing.

We dance for a little bit before I suggest we all go take shots. I pour all the girls a shot of vodka and we down them. "Another round." I shout and pour out another round of shots for everyone. They all roll their eyes at me but down the shots with me. I convince them to take a few more rounds of shots and then we go back to dancing.

We're jumping up and down and falling all over each other laughing. "Guys another round!" I drag them back to the table and pour another round of vodka shots. We all down them in seconds. "Another!" Brooke shouts grabbing the bottle from me and pouring us one more round.

After we down them Brooke goes to pour another round but Noah comes up and interrupts grabbing the bottle. "Alright thats it y'all are cut off how many shots have y'all had." "Aww come on don't be a party pooper we haven't had that many." Nicky giggles tripping over Brooke and grabbing at the bottle in Noahs hand. "Mhm and you just proved my point come one we're going home."

"Boooo!" I start and Jules, Brooke, and Nicky all join in. "Okay, Okay thats enough out of y'all." Noah picks up Nicky and throws her over his shoulder. He shouts for Asher, Jake, and Ethan and they come over.

"What the fuck Madison how much have you drank." Jake asks as I trip over my own feet and fall. Brooke laughs. "Jakey come on don't be a downer we've only had like what was it 8 rounds of shots?" "Jesus christ!" Jake mumbles under his breath as Brooke stumbles into him.

"Ethan grab Jules." Noah points at Jules who has wondered off and is talking to a group of girls.

"Oh my god I love your fit girl you look amazing you guys should come back to our house." She exclaims at the girls. They're all giggling. "Okay Jules you're done. We don't invite strangers to our house." Ethan throws her over his shoulder. "Sorry to interrupt ladies but its past her bedtime."

I'm laughing at Jules when I trip and bump into Asher. "Oh my god hey!" "Okay thats it come on." Asher tries to grab me. "No don't touch me I'm not going with you." "Madison cut it out come on you are wasted you need to go home." He reaches for me again.

"Why the fuck do you even care?" I go to storm off but he grabs me and throws me over his shoulder.

"Asher what the fuck put me down." I bang my fists on his back and kick my legs but it doesn't even seem to faze him.

At this point all four of the guys are walking down the street with one of us girls thrown over their shoulders all while we're giggling and yelling at them to walk faster.

When we get to the house the boys take us all straight to bed. Asher sets me down on my bed and takes off my shoes. He moves to leave. "Asher..." He looks up. "Why did you avoid me today?"

"You are far too drunk for this conversation go to sleep Mads." He walks out and closes the door gently behind him.

Before I can even take time to think of what he said sleep overcomes me.

Authors Note

Hey Y'all I'm back! I'm not totally sure how I feel about this chapter I'm still recovering from a little bit of jet lag lol so I don't think its my best but I wanted to get something out there for y'all.

I really wanted to bring awareness to what trauma bonds can look like. You can experience a trauma bond under any type of abuse whether it is verbal, emotional, or physical. I also wanted to show how sometimes episodes of depression can come out of nowhere. I want you all to know that my messages are always open and I am always here to listen. If you have experienced a trauma bond or any mental health issues I want you to know it is not your fault and you are not alone. You are enough and so incredibly loved.

Let me know your thoughts on this chapter!

chapter sixteen

I woke up to my head pounding. I feel a rush of nausea and run to the bathroom. Fuck I drank way too much last night.

We're leaving today so I have to pack up all of my things. I wish we could stay at the beach forever. Life seems so much simpler here but we have to get back to reality.

I made a decision that I was gonna go back to California and make things right with Cade and grab some more of my things. I felt like I owed him that and that maybe if I went back I would be able to get the closure I needed.

We packed up the car pretty quickly and split into our assigned cars except for the fact I traded places with Nicky so I wouldn't have to be around Asher.

I faked sleeping most of the way so that no one would talk to me or ask questions about why I switched. My head was pounding the whole way but closing my eyes helped. I could feel Noah's concerned glances through the rear view mirror but I ignored him. He's such a dad.

We only made one stop on the way home at a gas station for Ethan to pee and Noah ran in and grabbed us all water bottles except for Ethan he was cut off of liquids to avoid another bathroom stop.

When we finally made it home I went straight to my room to find a ticket to fly to California in the morning. I wanted to get it all over with before I chickened out. I booked my flight to leave at 9 am tomorrow and come back in 2 days. I packed a couple of things in my duffel bag and then prepared myself to give the news to Jake.

I walk over to his room and knock on the door. He shouts to come in and I take a deep breath before opening the door. Brooke is sitting on his bed laughing at him as he unpacks.

"Um Brooke would you mind giving us a second? I'm so sorry to interrupt." "Of course don't worry about it." She quickly leaves and shuts the door behind her.

"Mads whats up you've been acting off the past couple of days are you okay?" "Yes, yes, of course I'm okay I'm sorry I didn't mean to worry you I've just been tired I guess the move is catching up with me." I fake a laugh.

"Okay so what did you want to talk to me about?" "I umm I'm leaving tomorrow go back to California for a couple of days. I have some things I have to take care of."

"What things? Does it have anything to do with the things that happened that made you have to leave so abruptly?" He leans against his dresser and just stares at me waiting for my answer. I hate hiding things from him but I can't tell him.

"Um kind of I guess." I look down at my feet not wanting to meet his eyes. "Do you need someone to go with you?" I wish he would go with me but he can't see what my life was like before I came here.

"No I'll be fine I just have to grab a few things pay a few bills you know the usual boring moving shit." I laugh. "Okay if you say so." He shrugs his shoulders and I move to leave but he stops me.

"Mads you know you can be honest with me right? You know you don't have to hide anything from me." "Of course I do I'm not hiding anything."

"You promise?" I hesitate. "Of course."

"Mads I love you and I care about your wellbeing and I need you to know that you can talk to me about anything."

"I know Jakey and the same goes for you. Now enough of this cheesy gross stuff before I throw up in my mouth." We laugh and he pulls me in for a hug before letting me leave.

Jake must've told the rest of the house that I'm leaving in the morning because Noah goes all out for dinner making his famous chicken alfredo.

--- Possible ED TW ---

I force myself to finish a whole plate of it not wanting to offend Noah by not eating it. I'll just throw it up later it'll be fine I reassure myself. I have already gained a little bit of weight since being here and the last thing I want is for Cade to make a comment about it.

After dinner Noah brings out the brownies but I turn it down saying I'm full. I run up the stairs to bathroom.

I force my two fingers down my throat and watch as my dinner hits the toilet. My eyes start to tear up but I swallow it back refusing to allow myself to cry over it.

I take a few deep breaths and put a smile on my face before opening the bathroom door. I've gotten really good at faking smiles and feigning happiness.

As I walk out I bump into Asher. He reaches out and steadies me. "Madison why the fuck are you going to California in the morning?"

"Its really none of your business Asher. You clearly do not care about me so please just leave me the fuck alone." I try and brush past him but he stops me.

"You are not going to California I don't have a good feeling about this." "Asher you don't get to tell me what to do. I'm a grown adult I can take care of myself."

"If you can take care of yourself then stop being so reckless with your life. I can't just stand here and watch you go back to whoever gave you all those fucking bruises." "Nobody asked you too just leave me alone Asher."

I brush past him and he shouts after me. "You are being stupid Madison and you know it." I ignore him and keep walking to join everyone else in the living room. He doesn't know me. He has no right to try and tell me what to do.

Asher doesn't join us for the rest of the night but nobody questioned it. He's just being typical Asher going off on his own.

I decide to go to bed early because of my early flight in the morning. I give everyone a hug goodnight and head to bed. I double check that I have everything I need for my flight in the morning before taking a quick shower and letting sleep take over.

chapter seventeen

I wake to my alarm going off its 5 am. I get up and take a quick shower. I throw my hair up and apply a little makeup and put on a pair of jeans and the first sweatshirt I come across.

I hear a knock at my door. I open it to reveal Jake on the other side. "You ready?" He had agreed to drive me to the airport.

"Yeah let me just grab my stuff." I throw my backpack on my shoulders and reach for my duffel but Jake beats me to it. "I got it."

We're driving down the road in silence until Jake breaks it. "Have you thought about what you are going to do when you get back here?"

I turn to look at him. "What do you mean?" "Are you going to continue staying with us or were you thinking about trying to get an apartment?"

"Do you need me out?" "No of course not. I was actually going to ask if you wanted to move in permanently?"

"Jake I can't intrude on your life. This is your life your friends." "They're your friends too Mads. They all want you to stay but in the end its up to you. Your choice."

"They want me to stay?" My heart melts at that thought. "They don't even know me why would they want that?"

"They know you enough. They all love you." He responds. I just sit there contemplating what he said. "You don't have decide right now Mads Its just something to think about."

"Thanks Jake for everything." He just nods his head at me.

We sit in silence for the rest of the way until he pulls up to drop me off at the front of the airport.

"You know if you need me at all I'm just a phone call away okay?" "Okay" I swallow back my anxiety and get out. He grabs my duffel from the trunk and hands it to me. I give him a quick hug. I take one last deep breath before walking through the airport doors.

I send a quick text to Cade letting him know I'm coming. He always hated surprises because it meant he was out of control. I knew if I didn't tell him it would just make things worst.

Once I get through security I anxiously wait at my seat for them to start boarding.

It feels like hours had passed when I finally reached my seat and sat down. The truth was only one hour had passed but anxiety had made it feel like 5 hours.

I try and close my eyes and sleep but I can't sleep. I switch from watching movies on the airplane screen and reading my book the whole five hours on the plane.

When I finally get off the plane I call an uber and wait outside. A black SUV pulls up 30 minutes. I hesitate to get in because of m last experience with an uber but I know Cade won't pick me up so I force myself to get in.

The ride to Cade and I's apartment seems to drag on forever. When the driver finally pulls in front of the apartment complex Cade and I shared for 2 years memories come flooding back. I remember the first year before we moved into together how amazing he was. How he used to bring me coffee and flowers to my work.

When he would take me on dates. I told him once that I had wished we were in the regency era when they went to fancy balls. He laughed at me and told me I read too many books but later that weekend he surprised me by taking me to some ballroom dance class.

He used to be so romantic. He seemed almost perfect but then when we moved in together its like he flipped a switch. I don't know what I did to make him change.

I hesitate before getting out but I make my way up to the second floor and stop at the third door. I pull out my key and unlock it.

I step inside and Cades nowhere to be seen I let out a breath not realizing I had been holding it. I walk to our room and grab a big suitcase from the closet and start filling it up with all of my things.

A couple of thing are going to have to go in garbage bags to be donated. I bough a lot of things in New York so I don't really need much.

After the suitcase is full I walk to the office to pay off the lease I'm not going to continue paying for Cade to stay here.

When we first got the apartment we put the lease in my name because Cades credit score was shit. He had told me we would split the rent but he never did give me his share.

The lady at the office was nice and made things quick. We only had a few months left on the lease so I only had to pay a few months to get it paid off. I left 2 months to give Cade time to find another place.

I walked back to the apartment and Cade was waiting for me on the couch.

"Well look who decided to show up." He smiled but not a genuine smile but the type of smile that made the hair on your arms stand up.

I just stand there looking at him not sure what to say. "So you're just gonna give me the silent treatment now." He laughs. I still don't say anything. He stands up and walks up to me so he's standing less than an inch from my face.

"Say something." He shouts in my face. I flinch but I stand still almost like I'm frozen too scared to move.

"You're useless." He laughs and brings his hand back to slap me but I dodge it finally able to move.

That only makes him more angry. "You bitch." I look at him his eyes turn black his face is full of rage and I know whats coming. "I'm sorry Cade please don't I'm sorry." I cower in the corner trembling.

He stalks towards me. "So you're in New York for 2 weeks and you decide to be a little brave." As he gets closer my body trembles harder.

"I came to make things right." My voice breaks. He grabs me by my throat and picks me up off the floor. I feel my back being slammed into the wall. I can feel his gaze on my face but I refuse to look him in the eyes.

His fist comes flying into my jaw and then into my stomach over and over again.

"Look at me!" He shouts. I shake my head. "No." He throws me across the room and pain shoots up my back and legs as I hit the ground.

"Cade stop." I struggle to pull myself up to standing. "I'm leaving and you can't stop me. I'm done putting up with your shit."

"Fuck you Madison after everything I've done for you you're just gonna leave after everything we've been through." He sits down and puts his head in his hands.

"Cade I can't stay with you I can't keep letting you treat me this way. I thought that if I came back maybe you might've changed and I could leave peacefully and get some closure but clearly that's not going to happen." Tears well up in my eyes. "I paid off the lease you have 2 months to get out."

He shoots up from sitting. "What the fuck Madison!"

He starts to walk towards me but I grab the lamp off the table and hold it out between us.

"Don't come any closer Cade." My hands are shaking but I grip onto the lamp as if it's my life line which technically it kind of is.

"Madison stop you're being ridiculous this is ridiculous." He inches closer to me.

"Cade I'm serious don't come any closer to me I swear to god."

"Madison we can work this out like we always do I'll get my anger under control you can go to therapy. It's gonna be okay." His face softens and he looks at me almost the way he did when we first met.

I almost put the lamp down but I don't let myself. "No Cade, you say that every time and every time I believe you. Every time I think this time it'll be different but it never is. I keep holding out hope that you'll go back to being the person I fell in love with but that's never going to happen is it? Because that person wasn't real it was just a fucking persona." The tears fall blurring my vision.

"Madison you don't mean that you're being dramatic you just need to sleep."

"No Cade I need to leave and I am going to leave and if you try to stop me I swear to god this lamp will hit your head so hard you'll see stars."

I back into the room and grab my suitcase still holding the lamp out between us. I make my way to the door and grab his car keys and run out the door pulling my suitcase behind me the lamp still in my hands.

He's chasing after me but I got a head start. I get to his car and throw the suitcase in the trunk and get in the car locking the doors and driving off just as he comes around the corner.

"Madison!" I hear him yell behind me cursing but I don't look back I just keep driving.

My breaths come fast my body trembling.

I wipe my nose with my sleeve my eyes welling with tears.

I glance at my reflection in the rear view mirror. My eyes are puffy and red. Bruises are all over my face my hair is a wreck.

How did I let myself get here. How did I become this. Sadness and Anger overwhelms me. So much of my life was wasted.

I let all the tears out that I had been holding in. Sobs are shaking my body. Tears blurring my vision.

I stop at a red light and I just scream. I scream for my younger self that I never stood up for. I scream at myself for not walking away sooner.

My fists comes down banging on the steering wheel over and over again.

Pain is shooting up my wrist and arm and my throat is burning but I don't care.

I drive straight to the airport to see if I can switch my flight to leave tonight. I think when I thought I would be able to stay a couple of days I kind of hoped that maybe I would have a few good days with Cade and that would give me the closure that I thought I needed but that was a stupid thought.

I stop in the parking lot and take a deep breath trying to compose myself before I walk in.

I go straight to the customer service desk.

They luckily have a flight that'll leave in a couple hours that they had a seat left on.

I go ahead and get past security so that I can wait on the side that Cade can't get to me if he tries to stop me.

chapter eighteen

The whole plane ride I feel completely numb. It feels like I'm in a trance. I have my headphones on and just stare out the window playing the scene with Cade repeatedly in my head.

The flight attendant announces we're landing and like a robot completely unaware of my actions I make sure all my things are together and wait for the okay to get off the plane.

When I get off the plane I grab my checked bag from baggage claim and then scroll through my phone trying to figure out who to call. I go to call Jake but I change my mind I don't want him to see me like this I'm a mess and I can't call the girls or Asher.

I scroll through my phone until I come across Noah's name and I dial.

"Hello." His deep voice comes through the line. "Umm, Noah it's Madison." My voice is already starting to break. "I need help, Noah." the tears break through and I sob into the phone.

"Where are you?" The concern is breaking through his voice and I hate that I'm bothering him but I know he'll be able to handle the situation more reasonably then Jake. "I'm at the airport can you come alone?" "I'll be there in 10 minutes."

"Thank you, Noah."

After we hang up I go to the bathroom to try and pull myself together and then go to wait for him outside.

When he finally pulls up he immediately gets out. "Madison what the fuck happened to you?"

"I'm fine Noah I just want to go home." I pull my bags over to the car and he takes them from me and throws them in the trunk. He opens my door and waits for me to get in.

When I go to get in a sharp pain hits my stomach and I crumble. "Fuck." I moan clutching my stomach my vision going blurry.

Noah catches me and helps me into the car. "Fuck Madison are you okay?"

I nod my head. "I'm fine I'm just a little dizzy." "Madison your bleeding Jesus Christ." I look down to see blood dripping down my pants. "Fuck Noah I'm so sorry I'm gonna mess up your car." I'm sobbing now.

"Mads It's fine don't worry about that right now we're going to a hospital it's gonna be okay."

"Please don't tell Jake." I beg him. "Madison I'm calling Jake he needs to know."

I just nod my head not having the energy to argue with him. My vision starts to go black I hear him talking to Jake on the phone and then complete darkness hits.

--- Jakes Pov ---

I'm sitting at my desk answering emails when I look down and see an incoming call from Noah. I pick up. "Hey man whats up?"

"Jake you need to meet me at the hospital right now. I'm on my way there with Madison." "What the fuck do you mean? Why is she here? She wasn't supposed to get back until late tomorrow." I'm already grabbing my stuff and heading out the door.

"She asked me to pick her up from the airport alone she sounded shaken up on the phone and when I got there she wasn't doing well man. I'm not sure what happened but she had bruises and cuts all over her."

"Okay I'm on my way now." I jump in my car and speed out of the parking lot.

My heart is beating so fast my hands gripping the steering wheel what the fuck happened to her. I'm so pissed off right now but I'm trying to calm myself down. I can't go in there fuming I have to have a level head when I walk in there.

--- Noahs Pov ---

Madison is slipping in and out of consciousness. I'm speeding as fast as I can cars are honking at me but they're not really my concern at the moment.

Madison and I haven't really gotten a chance to know each other that well we don't really talk as much as everyone else but I've seen her with the others and I know they all love her.

I don't know why the fuck she called me but by the way she begged me not to tell Jake I'm assuming she's trying to hide whatever has been happening to her from Jake.

We finally pull into the parking lot of the emergency room and I pull up where the ambulances usually park not caring if they get pissed.

I walk around to Madisons side and quickly unbuckle her. When I pick her up she's completely limp.

I run inside. "I need a fucking doctor over here please."

Nurses rush over to me with a gurney and take Madison from my arms. They move quickly and rush Madison to a back room. I go to follow them but a nurse turns around and tells me I can't follow them I would have to wait.

Another nurse comes over and shows me to the waiting room and hands me a clipboard. "How are you related to the patient? "I'm not I'm just a friend her brother is on the way."

"Okay sir do you know how she acquired her injuries?" "No she was in California and when I picked her up from the airport was when I saw she was injured."

"Okay thank you sir when her brother gets here could you please ensure that he fills out those forms on that clipboard? Also I'm going to need to ask you to move your car we have ambulances coming in."

I nod my head. "What do I tell him when he gets here?" "We'll update you as soon as we hear anything as of right now all you can do is wait here." She smiles sympathetically at me. "Thank you." "Of course sir if you or her brother have any other questions the nurses station is just down the hall." I nod my head and thank her and she walks away.

I run outside and move my car to a parking spot.

When I get back inside I try and sit down in the chair but my leg keeps bouncing up and down not able to sit still I pace back and forth until I see Jake walking in.

I pause and wave him down and he jogs over. "Noah what the fuck is going on?"

"Jake I really don't know they haven't told me anything they just took her back a few minutes ago. All I know is when I picked her up she was covered in bruises and cuts and when she went to get in the car she cried out and grabbed her stomach. Blood started dripping down her legs and she lost consciousness soon after that and has been and out ever since."

"Fuck!" Jake yells causing an elderly couple sitting in the corner to glare at us. "I fucking told her if she needed anything to call me why the fuck did she not call me?"

"Jake I know you're pissed but you need to chill out you're causing a scene." I give a subtle jerk of my head pointing towards the elderly couple still glaring at us.

"They can fuck off." Jake mutters under his breath.

"Just sit here for a minute a take a breath I'm going to try and get us some coffee and call Nicky. The nurse needs you to fill out these forms." I point at a chair and hand him the clipboard.

Jake just nods his head and I leave him alone and head towards the cafeteria to find coffee.

Well I walk I debate what to tell Nicky I don't want to scare her but she should know I dial her number. She picks up on the first ring. "Hey baby whats up?" "Hi baby I have some news and I don't want you to worry because Jake and I are with her and I'm going to keep you updated."

"What is it?" "Its Madison baby. I picked her up from the airport she asked me to come alone and not tell anyone I didn't ask a lot of questions because I figured that wasn't what she needed at the time." I pause for a minute. "When I got there... Nicky... she was covered in bruises and cuts she started clutching her stomach like she was in a lot of pain and she umm started bleeding a shit ton." It takes everything in me to keep my voice from shaking as I tell her what I saw.

"Oh my god, oh my god." Her voice breaks and she pauses trying to process. "What should I do. What can I do." "Baby all we can do is wait at this point." "Okay baby keep me updated. Are you okay?"

I take a deep breath before answering. "I'm okay. Are you okay?" "I'm okay." Is all she says I can tell she's trying to stay strong but I know her heart is breaking for Madison. She adores Madison she treats her like a little sister.

We talk a little bit before hanging up. I'm grateful for the distraction I knew Nicky would help put me in a more calm stable mindset which I'll need. I have to be there for Jake.

I continue walking until I get to the Cafeteria and I grab Jake and I coffee and head back to where he's sitting filling out the paperwork.

He takes the coffee from me. "Thanks." I nod my head. "Any news?" He just shakes his head and I take a seat beside him sighing. I feel completely helpless and I hate it.

--- Authors Note (A Thank you!)

I know most of you probably won't read this because lets be honest here I rarely read the authors notes lol. But I just wanted to say thank you to all of you who have actively been coming back and reading each and every single one of my chapters. We have officially reached 1,000 reads and I couldn't be more grateful. I truly never thought this book would get to 500 reads let alone 1000. I am absolutely amazed by y'alls continued support, kindness, and patience you all have showed me. I also want to thank those who have been commenting, voting, and adding my book to your reading lists. That means the absolute world to me and has kept me extremely motivated to keep writing and keep getting chapters out for you guys. Thank you so much guys you all are amazing.

Reminder: You are enough and you are so incredibly needed and loved. Please if you need someone to talk to. If you are struggling please reach out to someone. You do not have to go through this alone. You are not a burden. You deserve to be heard and your struggles and your feelings are valid. As always my messages are always open. No judgement and no questions asked. :)

chapter nineteen

I open my eyes my vision is blurry I blink a couple of times and try and lift my head. I look around I'm in a room with machines and wires beside me the walls are completely white.

I know this place all too well. Hospitals all look the same completely plain and dreary but I personally didn't mind it because growing up I quickly learned that if I was here I was safe my Dad or Cade wouldn't hit me around doctors and nurses.

A nurse comes in interrupting my thoughts. "Hello Madison my name is Tara do you know why you're here?" I shake my head. "Your friend Noah brought you in with severe injuries. Can you tell me how you got them?" I shake my head again.

She frowns. "Okay, that's okay sweetie I'm just going to take your vitals and a doctor will be here shortly." She grabs my arm and starts taking my blood pressure.

After she leaves an hour later an older man comes in wearing a white coat. "Hello, Madison I'm Dr Stephan Neal I was the doctor on call when your friend brought you in. Whats your pain level right now."

"About a 7. What happened?" I grimace as I try and sit up. "Well that's what I was hoping you'd be able to tell me." Flashbacks run through my mind. Cade did this but I won't tell them that.

I shake my head. "Hmm well you came in with a couple broken ribs a strained wrist a concussion and an alarming amount of bruises and cuts." "How can that be when I got on the plane I felt completely fine."

"In cases that involve such traumatic injuries victims will often go into shock which causes them to not be able to feel the full extent of their injuries. When you got off the plane you came out of shock and felt all of it at once causing you to lose consciousness."

"Madison theres one more thing we need to discuss." He takes a deep breath and sits down in the chair next to me. "Were you aware you were pregnant?" "No."

"When was the last time you were intimate with someone." "2 months ago."

"You were about 6 weeks pregnant." "Were?" "You lost the baby." "No!"

"Madison your injuries were too traumatic that the baby could not have survived there was nothing you could have done. The blood and the stomach cramps was you having a miscarriage."

I barely hear his voice my thoughts were too loud how could I have let this happen. I allowed him to do this I should have never gone back. This was all my fault.

"No, no, no what have I done." I sob tears were falling down my face so fast soaking my hospital gown but I didn't care. "I lost my baby." I sob harder.

"Madison can you tell me who did this?" I shake my head my breaths coming harder and faster. I'm hyperventilating my whole body trembling. I'll never get away from him. I feel a needle prick me and my whole body relaxes before I lose all consciousness.

(POSSIBLE TW - talk of domestic abuse and rape-)

--- Jakes Pov ---

I'm pacing the waiting room when a doctor approaches us. "Jake?" "Yes thats me." "We have news on your sister."

"Okay go ahead." The doctor looks hesitantly at Noah. "He's fine to hear anything you have to say he was the one that brought her in."

"Your sister has an extensive amount of injuries. She had 2 broken ribs a sprained wrist an alarming amount of several cuts and bruises we suspect domestic abuse." A shaky breath escapes and it takes everything in me to remain standing. Noah squeezes my arm trying to offer his silent support.

"Do you have any idea who might've done this?" "I uhh I don't know."

"We took a look at her medical history and she has come in an alarming amount of times starting at the age of 3 for similar injuries."

"At 3 that can't be right are you sure?" "Yes sir. But theres more." "Okay."

"Your sister she was 6 weeks pregnant she lost the baby. Because of her medical history as well as the extent of your sisters injuries we suspect sexual abuse sir but we can't be for certain unless we do some tests but we need her permission to conduct those tests."

"What are you saying?" "Sir your sister might've been raped by whoever was abusing her."

I collapse in the chair behind me. My eyes well up with tears. I was supposed to protect her why wasn't I there. Why did she not call me. My head falls into my hands and I allow myself to cry for my sister and what she's been through. Sobs shake my entire body. I feel Noahs hand on my back silently telling me he's there for me.

When I look up I see his eyes are full of tears too. The doctor is still there. "Is she awake?" "She was we had to give her a sedative she was on the verge of a panic attack when we told her about the baby so she's asleep now. You may go in and see her now if you would like."

I nod my head and he motions for me to follow him. Noah stays back.

When I walk in the room and see her lying there hooked up to several machines looking completely helpless it takes everything in me not to start crying again but I don't allow myself to I have to be strong for her.

--- Ashers Pov ---

I'm at the gym taking my anger out on my sparring partner. Boxing helps me manage my anger and my emotions in some ways it's my escape. I hear my phone going off for the thirteenth time.

"Pause." My sparring partner rolls his eyes but walks away to get water.

I look down at my phone Noahs blowing up my phone he never does that so I pick up. "Noah whats wrong."

"Are you with anyone?" "No I'm at the gym why whats going on?" "Something has happened to Madison I'm..." "What the fuck do you mean something happened to her." "Let me finish. I'm with Jake at the hospital I'm not going to tell you anything else because if she wants everyone to know she should be the one to tell them."

"Just tell me whats going on Noah!" "I can't do that Asher I need you to calm the fuck down I called you because I need you to tell everyone and get the girls to the hospital. She's sleeping now but I think when she wakes up it'll help her if she sees the girls."

"Okay." Is all I say to Noah before hanging up. Fuck what is wrong with her I told her not to go to California why didn't she listen to me.

I dial Nickys phone. "Hey Ash." "Hey can you make sure you and the girls and Ethan are ready to go when I get there? I'll be there in about 15." "Are we going to see Madison?" "Yeah." "Okay we'll be ready."

chapter twenty

When I get to the house Ethan and the girls are waiting outside. They all get in not saying a word. We ride in silence my hands grip the steering wheel and my thoughts run through my brain.

"Do you know what happened?" Jules hesitantly breaks the silence. I shake my head."Noah wouldn't tell me. "That means it's bad," Brooke says, staring through the window.

"She's going to be okay she's in good hands," Nicky responds in a definite way.

"You don't know that Nicky. You can't always assume the best in every situation." I bite back at her. "I know that." is all she says before falling silent now I feel bad. "Fuck!" I yell slamming my fist on the steering wheel.

"It's gonna be fine dude you need to chill," Ethan says squeezing my shoulder. "I warned her not to go to California. I fucking told her not to go."

Everyone stays silent the rest of the way. When we walk in we get visitor stickers at the front desk and get told the room number.

Noah meets us halfway. "Hey baby." Nicky gives him a quick hug and we all follow him to the room.

Before we walk in Noah stops us. "Before you go in I have to warn you its not going to be a pretty sight whoever did this to her beat her up pretty good. They gave her a sedative so she's sleeping now she should be awake in a couple hours. The doctor told us as well as they already told her she had a miscarriage."

Jules gasps. Noah continues talking but I don't hear him. She was pregnant what the fuck.

"Her emotional state it's going to be all over the place but we just have to offer our support and be strong for her and Jake." Noah finishes and everyone nods their agreement before he opens the door.

When the door opens nobody could have prepared for the sight that greeted us. She lay asleep on the hospital bed hooked up to several machines and monitors. Her right wrist was bandaged cuts and bruises covered her arms. One of her eyes was swelling.

Jake looks up at us he looks like a wreck. He has this devastated helpless look on his face. His eyes puffy and red and bags under his eyes making it seem like he hasn't slept in days.

"I need a minute." Is all I say before leaving the room and closing the door behind me. My breaths come fast and heavy. "Fucking hell." I mutter to myself my hands come up rubbing my face.

I look down at my hand it's shaking. It never shakes. I hear someone step out of the room behind me. "You alright man?" It's Ethan.

I just shake my head. "Who could do this? What kind of fucking coward would do this to her?"

"I don't know." Is all Ethan can say.

"To Madison of all people. She didn't deserve this nobody does. She's been nothing but kind to every single person."

I turn around to face Ethan. Tears are rolling down his face.

"Are you okay?" Ethan just shakes his head but takes a deep breath composing himself. "Let's go back in and be there for Jake and the girls."

I knew this might have been hitting a little too close to home for Ethan. He doesn't talk about it a lot but growing up his dad was a raging alcoholic and had extreme anger issues. Often his dads anger was taken out on Ethan when he was younger.

I know not to push him so I just nod my head and follow him back in.

Nicky's sitting on Noah's lap trying to hide the tears streaming down her face. Jules is sitting next to Madison's bed holding her hand tears forming in her eyes.

Brookes holding Jakes hand and Jake squeezing it like it's his life line like it's the only thing holding him together.

Ethan sits next to Jules and takes her other hand in his. I take a seat next to Jake and Brooke. All we can do at this point is wait.

—- Madison's Pov —-

I woke up and looked around the whole group was here all asleep expect Asher.

He sat in the chair staring at me. When he notices I'm awake he come closer "Hey Mads how are you feeling?"

"I'm okay." I'm not but he doesn't need to know that.

"Everyone's here." "Of course we are. Do you want me to get the doctor are you in any pain?"

"No don't leave please."

"Okay." He drags his chair closer to the bed. "Do you wanna tell me what happened?"

"Nothing happened." "Clearly something did Madison I'm not stupid."

"I'm fine." My voice breaking as I say that. I'm not doing a great job of convincing him of it.

"You're not." "I am." "Are you trying to convince me or you?" He scoffs.

I shake my head at him. "Just let it go." "Even if I let it go Mads you know Jake won't. You're going to have to tell someone eventually."

"Just please let it go." "I will for now. Do you need anything?"

"Water?" I ask hesitantly. He nods his head and grabs the pitcher and refills my cup.

I reach for the cup with my left hand because of my right hand being sprained. My hand shaking struggling to get a hold of the cup. "Fuck."

"Here let me do it." He brings the cup to my lips and tips it for me to drink.

"Thank you." He nods his head setting the cup down on the table beside me. "Anytime."

He sits down next to me and just looks at me for a minutes. "Mads I uhh..."

"Madison you're awake." Jake wakes up and jumps out of his chair interrupting us.

"I'll go get the doctor." Asher stands up leaving the room.

"How are you feeling?" Jake asks. "I'm fine Jake.""We have a lot to talk about."

Just then the doctor walks in thankfully interrupting Jake.

I'm not ready to tell him everything yet.

"Madison how are you feeling?" Doctor Neal asks while washing his hands at the sink.

I feel like I've been asked that 12 times already and not once have I given an honest answer.

"I'm fine." I answer. Doctor Neal looks around. "I'm going to have to ask everyone to leave the room." They all had woken up when Doctor Neal had come in and so they all nod their heads and quickly leave.

"Madison we have a few things to discuss."

"Okay." "Because of the extent of your injuries as well as your medical history we have reason to believe you have been a victim of domestic abuse is that true?"

I hesitantly nod my head. "Okay because of the domestic abuse we have to ask have you been a victim of sexual abuse?"

A broken sob escapes from my lips. "Yes." I almost whisper it it's so quiet.

"How long ago was the last time?" "2 months ago." He looks up at me at that his eyes full of sympathy at that. "Because it was that long ago a rape kit will not pick up any evidence. However we can get the police involved in order to press charges on the assault and issue a restraining order we just need a name."

"No." "No?" "Please I don't want to talk to the police I don't want to press charges I just want to go home."

"Okay then I will get a nurse in here and get you discharged we have no other reasons to keep you here any longer. We just are going to ask you to take it easy for the next couple of weeks."

I nod my head in agreement and he leaves. After he leaves everyone walks in.

"What did he say?" Jake asks. "All he said was that I am ready to be discharged a nurse will be in shortly."

"That's all he said?" Asher asks. "Yep." "Hmm." Is all he says not believing me but he lets it go.

The nurse comes in and gets me discharged as quickly as possible and they roll me out in a wheelchair despite my arguments.

chapter twenty one

I t's been a few days since I was discharged when we had gotten back to the house Jake and Noah helped me to my room and for most of the day, they left me alone.

A couple of times each day someone would come in the room and try and get me to eat but I would turn them away and they'd leave. I just wanted to sleep. I liked sleep because when I was asleep I couldn't think.

I couldn't think about the fact that I allowed myself to be abused and that I allowed my baby to die. I couldn't think about the fact that maybe the baby was better off dead than my child.

Because those thoughts would then make me think of my mother the woman I swore never to become but looking back I realize she is exactly who I became.

A woman who knew the hand her children were being dealt by her husband the same man that abused and used her and yet she did nothing. She made no action to leave and I guess I somewhat understand why she didn't because I did the same thing.

When you fall so deeply in love with someone you ignore all the bad days and focus on the good. You hold out hope that one day there will be no bad days but that day never comes. Because the good days are always an act. An act to keep your hopes just high enough that you'll stay.

The good days will always come when you threaten to leave because when those days come and he shows kindness and gentleness, you'll start to remember the beginning of the relationship when that was all that he showed you and all thoughts of leaving are erased from your mind.

I wish I would have left sooner. I should have left sooner because then maybe it wouldn't hurt as much as it does right now.

I close my eyes and try and block out the thoughts rushing through my brain. But sleep never comes the thoughts don't stop.

Finally I get up and make my way to the bathroom to take a shower. Showers always help me escape.

I let the water run over my hair and my shoulders. All of the sudden my vision gets blurry and my my mind starts to blank everything around me seems like its moving in slow motion. I feel my legs giving out and I collapse. Everything is dark.

--- Ashers Pov ---

Everyone went out to go get something to eat and to get out of the house Jake was going to stay behind to keep an eye on Madison but I knew he needed a break so I offered to stay back instead.

This thing with Madison was taking its toll on everyone but no one would admit it.

I'm focused on the tv in front of me when I hear a crash from upstairs. "Fuck" I race up the stairs and check her room. She's not in there so I race to the bathroom.

When I open the door steam comes from the shower the water still running. I pull back the curtain and she's huddled on the floor. She looks so fragile like skin and bones.

When was the last time she ate. She's been refusing food for days. I grab a towel and wrap it around her averting my eyes and pick her up in my arms.

I go to take her to her bed but I remember her sheets probably haven't been changed for awhile so I take her to my bed.

"Mads come on love open your eyes." I lightly pat her face and she opens her eyes. "Good girl."

"What happened?" she whimpers. "Its alright you just passed out in the shower you're okay."

I set her down and pull the covers over her. I grab one of my sweatshirts. "Arms up there you go." I pull it over her head. I run downstairs and grab some leftover soup Nicky had made and a bottle of water.

When I get back up the stairs she's just staring blankly at the wall curled up in a ball.

"Alright Mads sit up you gotta eat something." "No."

"Don't give me shit right now Madison you're fucking eating. You haven't eaten in days."

"No I don't deserve it just leave me alone Asher!" She bite back a sob breaking free. "Oh Mads no no don't say that."

She sobs harder. "I killed my baby. It's my fault. I don't deserve to eat." She whimpers.

I kneel in front of her. "Madison look at me." I grab her chin and force her to look me in the eyes. Her eyes are red and puffy and it kills me. The bags under her eyes showing she hasn't slept the past couple of days probably scared of having nightmares.

"Baby you did not kill your child none of this is your fault you didn't ask for any of this." I sit her up and wipe her eyes.

"Open." I put the spoon full of soup to her lips and she hesitantly opens. "Thats my girl."

I put the water to her lips and she drinks.

After she finished her soup and water I go to leave but she stops me. "Ash." She whispers it I barely hear it.

"Yes?" I turn around and face her. "Please don't leave me alone. Please stay."

"Okay." I put the dishes back on the nightstand and get in the bed beside her. Dirty dishes are the last of my worries.

Her body snuggles up against me and within minutes quiet snores escape her and I know she's asleep.

I allow myself to close my eyes for just a minute I haven't slept much the last couple of days either.

--- Jakes Pov ---

When we get home Asher is nowhere to be seen. I run upstairs to check on Madison. She's gone. What the fuck.

I run out shouting for Noah. "Noah Madisons gone!"

"Shut up Jake." Nicky shushes me from where she's peaking into Ashers room. "They're both in here sound asleep."

"Mads is asleep?" "See for yourself." Nicky opens the door wider. Madison is sound asleep with her head resting on Ashers chest.

"Lets leave them alone." Nicky ushers me out.

chapter twenty two

I woke up to see Asher lying next to me watching me sleep. "You're still here?"

"I didn't want to leave you alone in case you had another nightmare." He responds as he reaches beside him to grab his phone.

"Oh."I quickly move to get up. Don't get attached Madison. "You didn't have to do that."

"I wanted to."

I think about that statement for a minute just sitting at the edge of the bed. We both sit in silence before I finally break it a couple of minutes later. "Why?"

"Hmm?" He asks absently scrolling through his phone. I swallow back my hesitation. "Why did you want to?"

"I guess I care." He laughs uncomfortably still scrolling through his phone. I shift to turn around and face him.

"Why do you care? What do you get from caring?" "Nothing." He finally puts his phone down staring at me his forehead wrinkled in confusion. "Mads what is this about?"

I take a deep breath letting out a laugh. "Nothing." I force myself to stand up and move one foot in front of the other back to my room.

One thing I learned from a very young age is that everyone always has a secret agenda. Nobody is in it just because. They all want something. You are only worth what you can give that is where your sole value comes from and If anyone tells you differently they're lying to you.

"Madison wait whats wrong why are you acting like this?" Asher asks reaching out to grab my arm to stop me.

I look down at his grasp on my arm panic filling my eyes. I freeze in fear. He sees the look on my face and immediately drops his grip and I run out.

I keep running until I get to my room. I close the door and lock it behind me.

I sit on my bed hugging my knees to my chest rocking back and forth.

My breathing is coming heavier. Stop it Madison you are fine pull yourself together. You can do this.

I try and slow my breathing.

I don't understand why I'm like this I feel horrible that I keep pushing Asher away but I can't talk to him.

I can't open myself up to more pain.

TRIGGER WARNING

I get up and stumble around my room bumping into things along the way. My vision going blurry.

Cades voice rings in my head. You are worthless. Nobody is going to put up with your shit the way I do. Your own parents hated you.

I fall to my knees and search under my bed. There it is. Jakes pocket knife. I had seen it a couple days ago and took it. I couldn't bring myself to use it but that was then.

I grab a piece of paper from my notebook and a pen.

I walk to my bedroom door and peak out waiting to make sure it is clear before stumbling towards the bathroom door and step in locking the door behind me.

I stop for a minute and stare at my reflection. I am ugly and broken. Cade was right. Who would love me?

Asher doesn't really care. Jake doesn't really care I'm just a burden on all of them.

They won't care if I'm gone they would be relieved.

I take a deep breath before turning around and turning the water on.

I watch as the tub fills up. Tears filling my eyes and I grab the piece of paper and my pen and force myself to write.

All I manage to get on the paper is two words. I'm sorry.

I leave the paper on the counter.

I take another deep breath and force myself to get in the tub. I'm finally going to have peace. No more nightmares. No more pain. No more fear. No more counting calories and throwing up. No more Cade. I'll be done. I'll be free.

One more deep breath and I take the knife to my wrist shutting my eyes. Silent tears escaping as I cut across my skin pushing deeper and deeper.

One last deep breath as I move to the other wrist.

I drop the knife and rest my head against the tub. I can feel the blood dripping down my arms but I don't let myself look I keep my eyes closed waiting for it all to fade away.

--- Ashers Pov ---

It's been a few hours since my interaction with Madison. I was debating whether or not I should try and talk to her but I forced myself to leave her alone.

I shift to lay on my bed and shut my eyes. I hear Jake in the hallway. "What the fuck theres water all over the floor in here."

I ignore him and shut my eyes again. Jake starts banging on the bathroom door. "Who the fuck is in there? turn the water off."

When he continues banging on the door I finally pull myself out of bed and walk out into the hall to see whats going on.

As soon as I step into the hallway my socks become soaked. What the fuck theres water everywhere.

I storm over to where Jake is still banging on the bathroom door. "What the fuck is going on?"

Jake sighs. "I don't know I just got home from work and the hallway is completely flooded and the bathroom doors locked but nobodys answering.

"Its only me and Madison home and shes been in her room."

Jake walks over to Madisons room and knocks on the door. No answer. He opens the door revealing an empty room.

"Fucking hell." I run back to the bathroom and feel above the door for the spare key and pray Madison just fell asleep and shes okay.

I find the key and hurry and unlock the door and throw it open.

I freeze at the sight that greets me. Madison is completely submerged in the tub blood and water flowing from the tub covering the floor.

Jake comes up behind me. "Oh my god Madison."

I jump into action and pull her out of the water feeling for a pulse. "Jake call 911."

Jake just nods his head and stumbles out fumbling for his phone. I hear him talking to an operator.

I reach for a towel and wrap it around madisons wrists cradling her in my arms. Her pulse is weak but its there.

"Madison stay with me baby I got you. You're gonna be okay." I rock her in my arms gripping the towel trying to stop the blood.

Jake comes back in. "They uhh they said they're sending an ambulance."

"When will it be here?" I ask.

Jake just stares at Madisons unconcios face not answering. "JAKE!" I shout pulling his attention back to me. "When will it be here?"

"They umm they said five minutes."

"Okay go wait outside in the driveway for them so you can tell them where we are."

Jake nods his head and takes one more look at Madison before hesitantly leaving.

I take a deep breath. Madisons going to be fine. Everything's going to be fine. Stay strong for Jake.

I hear footseteps running up the stairs and Jakes voice. "They're in here."

Two paramedics come in. One of them takes Madison from me and puts her on a gurney feeling for her pulse. Another pulls out gauze and tape and starts wrapping up her wrists to keep her from losing anymore blood.

They take her out to the ambulance and me and Jake follow. "Jake ride with her in the ambulance I'll follow ya'll."

Jake just nods his head and I run back inside grabbing my keys and my phone.

chapter twenty three

-- Ashers Pov ---

It's been hours since we've been updated on Madison. The others all came to wait with us as soon as I called Noah to tell him what happened.

I needed Noah to be here if not for me but for Jake. I'm trying to stay calm for Jake but my mindset right now is just as all over the place as Jake's is so I'm thankful Noah got here when he did.

Nothing seems to faze Noah he seems to always be in a calm state of mind very much unlike me.

I'm pacing the floor when a nurse approaches us.

"Madison is stable. However, she lost a tremendous amount of blood we had to give her a transfusion. She's sleeping now but you can go in and see her."

We all nod our heads and follow her to Madisons room. There she lays sleeping peacefully as if she didn't just give us all the biggest scare.

I freeze in the doorway before walking out. I can't do this. This is all my fault.

I keep walking until I'm outside and finally stop at a bench. I allow my body to collapse on the bench resting my head in my hands.

I hear footsteps approaching and someone taking a seat next to me. "Are you okay?" I look up to meet Nickys eyes.

She smiles but its not a happy smile her eyes betray her. "Are you okay?" I ask her. She just shakes her head. "I asked you first."

"This is all my fault." "Why do you say that?" I shrug my shoulders. "I don't know I just feel like it is. She was acting weird this morning I must've done something. Somehow I always seem to fuck things up." I let out a defeated laugh.

"Ash this is not your fault. Madison has been through a tremendous amount of trauma and she feels stuck and alone and theres nothing any of us can do until she feels she can trust us. Which I know you don't want to hear this but It's going to take time." She puts her hand on my shoulder and squeezes it. "You can't fix everyone Ash and you can't blame yourself."

"Thanks Nicky." "Anytime."

"Now back to you are you okay?" I ask her.

She takes a deep breath. "I'm okay. I'm scared and shaken up but I'm okay." She tries to smile but tears well up in her eyes.

"No you're not." I say. She laughs. "Well I don't think anyone really is right now." I nod my head in agreement. "I just feel so helpless."

"I know but all we can do is go up there and be strong for Jake. He needs us right now." Nicky says standing and puts her hand out for me to take it.

I take it and she drags me up and we both start walking back to the room.

--- Madisons Pov ---

I open my eyes my vision blurry I blink until my vision becomes normal. I look around the room I'm in.

White walls, bed, metal chairs against the wall, an old tv mounted. I know where I am.

Jakes jerks up out of his chair when he sees my eyes open. "Mads you're awake how are you feeling?"

I just stare at him. "Why am I here?" "Madison don't you remember?"

"I know what happened that is why I'm asking why am I here?" My eyes fill with tears blurring my vision once again.

Jake just looks at me his sadness evident in his eyes as he realizes what I'm asking.

"I'm going to get the doctor." Noah stands up squeezing Jakes arm as he passes by. As he walks out I see Asher and Nicky walking in.

Asher catches my eye and I quickly look away.

"Madison..." Jake starts but the doctor comes in interrupting him. It's the same doctor I had last time.

"Madison its good to see you're awake." Dr. Neal says approaching me. "How are you feeling are you in any pain?"

"I'm fine." "Hmm." He takes my wrist in his hand checking my pulse. "Any chills or nausea?" I shake my head. "Alright while we are going to keep you here overnight to monitor your vitals and because this was an attempted suicide I had to page psych a psychiatrist will be by talk to you in a little bit and will be able to better help you with deciding what your next steps are from here."

I nod my head and roll over to face the wall. I don't want to see all the faces that I know I let down. I don't want to see their pity either.

"Thank you Dr. Neal." I hear Jake say and then I hear the door open and close and someone walk out. Not even a few minutes later the door opens and closes again and someone walks in.

"Hello everyone. I'm Dr. Avery." A woman's cheery voice says. "I'm going to ask all friends and family to leave the room for a little bit while I talk to Madison alone." I hear chairs scraping and footsteps as they all make their way out and the door closes behind them.

I hear Dr. Avery pull a chair closer to my bed. "Hi Madison. How are you?" I don't say anything. I don't know how to answer that question.

"I understand that all of this might seem overwhelming and I know you have been through quite a lot. I looked through your file. I am just here to help Madison but I can't help you if you don't talk to me." She says.

I take a deep breath and turn to face her. Tears streaming down my face. "Madison I understand you recently had a miscarriage do you want to tell me about that?" I shake my head tears coming faster.

"Madison." I take a deep breath. "I'm sorry." "You have nothing to apologize for you have been through several traumatic events it's only natural that you feel closed off." I nod my head.

"Can you tell me about what lead up to making you feel like you wanted to end your life?"

I hesitate. "Its okay take your time." I nod my head and take deep breaths trying to calm myself down. "I uh I don't really know. I just kind of feel useless." my voice shakes. "I feel like all ever do is let people down." Dr. Avery nods. "Has someone told you this or said something to make you feel this way." I slowly nod my head. "Do you want to talk about that?" I shake my head.

"Okay thats okay. I have to ask you a couple more questions and then i'll get out of your hair." She says writing something down on her clipboard. "Would you feel safe going home?" I nod my head. "I need you to answer the questions verbally sweetheart." "Yes" I say quietly. "

"Do you feel if you went home you would attempt suicide again or attempt to harm yourself in anyway?" "No" I force myself to answer out loud.

"Okay that's all then sweetheart. I'm gonna step outside and talk to your brother and then we'll come inside and all talk together."

I nod my head and she leaves.

--- Jakes Pov ---

Dr. Avery comes out shutting the door behind her and approaches me.

"How is she?"

"She's okay. I do want to discuss some things with you. I want you to understand how sensitive this situation is and I want to make sure you fully understand that Madison attempted suicide." I nod my head not trusting my voice.

"Because it was attempted suicide we have to talk about possibly getting her committed. However I don't believe that would be the best option for her. Madison has been through an incredible amount of trauma and a non familiar environment is going to just put her under more stress."

"I agree I strongly feel like my sister would do better under my care and I'm sure my friends would be more than happy to help out." I let a breath of relief I was afraid they would commit her.

"Well I am glad to hear that. However you have to understand this is not going to be an easy task. Madison will have to be placed under a 24/7 watch. I'm going to prescribe some antidepressants for her to take home. I expect you to ensure she takes them. I also am going to have to enforce mandatory counseling. She will need to find a therapist within 2-3 weeks or she will have to be committed."

"I understand ma'am thank you."

chapter twenty four

I rolled back over to face the wall when Dr. Avery left. I didn't want to face the others when they came back in. Tears were streaming down my face silent sobs shaking my body.

This wasn't supposed to happen. I am not supposed to be here still.

I hear the door open and close. Only one person's footsteps echo as they move closer to me.

I hear Jakes's heavy sigh as he takes a seat in the chair Dr. Avery had just been sitting in.

"Mads look at me." I hesitantly turn over to face him. "Why did you do it?"

"Please don't make me answer that." I whimper tears coming down faster.

"Madison please talk to me what is going on? It's me your big brother. You used to be able to tell me everything."

"Not everything." I sob. He looks up and stares at me confused. "The way mom and dad treated me wasn't what you think." I slowly try and get up to a sitting position. Jake jumps out of his seat and helps to prop me up. Once I'm settled he stares at me expectantly.

"Dad umm he... he used to. " I look down at my lap not knowing how to continue. "He what?" Jake prompted.

"He would hit me Jake." I blurt out. Jake looks at me shocked. "Dad would never do that to you he loved you he was always giving you gifts and getting you whatever you wanted."

"It was a show Jake." I say trying to wipe the tears away but it was no use. "What happened in California?" Jake prompts me to continue.

"My ex boyfriend Cade. He had a temper I guess you could say. He did the same thing dad did. I guess daughters do try and find a man just like their dad." A sad laugh escapes me. I look up to see Jakes reaction. He's not laughing anger is all over his face his fists clenched. "Madison did he rape you?"

I look down at my lap again my face turning red. I don't answer his question. "Madison?" I nod my head.

"Did dad?" I nod my head again. "Madison look at me." I look up to meet his eyes. Unshed tears and anger is clear in his eyes. "Why didn't you tell me?" "I didn't want to let you down." I look back down.

"Madison you could never let me down none of this was your fault. I'm so sorry I wasn't there to protect you. I should've been there." Tears are streaming down his face now too. I've never seen my brother cry thats how I know this is bad. Seeing him cry only makes me start crying harder.

"What is his name?" He asks his fists clenched.

My first instinct is to protect him but I am tired of protecting him. "Cade Parker."

He nods his head. "Was the baby his?" Another nod from me. "Madison I swear to god He is going to pay for what he did. Dad may not have but Cade will."

"Jake it's too late Dr. Neal told me it was too late to get a rape kit the evidence is gone we have nothing on him except text messages. The most we can do is get a restraining order on him."

"Send me the screenshots of the texts." he says standing up. He moves to open the door allowing the rest of the group to pile in.

*********** (Time Jump) *************

The rest of the group had gone back to the house. Jake was gonna come and stay the night but Asher volunteered and with a lot of convincing Jake finally agreed to go home and sleep because he had work in the morning.

I was watching whatever shit was on the old as fuck tv and Asher was sitting in his chair scrolling through his phone but I kept feeling his eyes on me.

I let out a breath. "Asher just ask me what you want to ask me."

He looks at me and just stares for a second before hesitantly asking. "Why did you do it?"

I look down at my lap not wanting to face his searching stare.

"Thats the question of the hour." I laugh trying to distract him.

"Madison." He says staring me down.

"I know I know." I glance up into his eyes for a second before looking back down at my lap.

"Do you ever feel like life shouldn't be this tiring when your this young?" I laugh.

He doesn't answer.

"My whole life has been about surviving. Just staying alive and getting through the next day. But what was it all for? What if I just stopped trying to survive and allowed myself to let it all go."

He still doesn't say anything but I can hear him shifting in his seat.

"I don't have anything else to live for so why would I continue to live. All I ever do is let everyone down. Nobody cares about me they pretend they do but I know the truth. Everyone wants something from you. Theres no such thing as unconditionial love and I am tired of searching after something that does not exist." I slump into my bed.

"Thats not true Madison."

I laugh at him. He has no idea.

"What happened in California Madison who did this to you who the fuck made you feel this way? He asks staring at me.

"His name is Cade."

"How long had this been going on?"

"Two years with him my entire life with my dad."

"Your dad?"

I just nod my head.

"What did they do to you Madison?"

"They both had alcohol issues." I breathe in deeply before continuing. "Somehow when they were drunk I always found some way to piss them off. They would hit and kick me and choke me over and over again until

I was so weak that there would be no way I could fight back they would force me down and they umm..." I sob not being able to continue.

Asher gets up and sits on the edge of my bed pulling me into his arms. "Its okay you're safe now." Is all he says over and over again as I sob and he rubs my back making me sob even harder.

I've never ever felt someone try and comfort me .

chapter twenty five

It's been a month now since the incident. It's hard to know how to act after everything that has gone down everyone walks on eggshells around me and I hate it but I guess I would too if I were in the same situation as them.

I walk out of my room to hear the usual Taylor Swift music blaring through the house while Nicky cooks dinner.

"Hey love how are you feeling?" Nicky asks smiling. I look around and see everyone staring at me. "God can y'all just act normal let it go I almost fucking died so what." blurts out of my mouth. fuck. I freeze I did not mean to let that slip. "I'm so sorry Nicky I didn't mean that."

Nicky just stands there jaw dropped everyone is completely silent just staring at me you could hear a pin drop until the silence is broken by Jules. She breaks down hysterically laughing almost, falling out of her chair while poor Ethan, sitting next to her, is taking the brunt of her fist.

Everyone soon joins in the laughter. "Y'all are all nuts. I live in a house with a bunch of crazies." I shake my head turning to walk away." "Wait Mads... it's just... we've never... seen... you... that angry..." Jules breathes out still dying laughing wiping tears from her eyes. "Did you see Nicky's face? Oh my god man I needed that."

I keep walking until I close my bedroom door behind me. The truth is I say they don't know how to act around me but I don't know how to act around them either.

My brothers been gone everyday since that accident probably avoiding me.

I'm lost in my thoughts when I hear a knock on the door and Ashers head peaks in.

"Hey we're getting out of the house tonight be ready to go by 7." His head disappears and the door closes before I can say no or ask him where we're going.

I sit on my bed and just stare at the wall ahead of me.

When 7 hits I still haven't moved from my spot on the bed Nicky tried to get me to come down for dinner but I told her I wasn't hungry.

I hear a knock on the door and prepare an excuse in my mind on why I shouldn't go out with Asher tonight.

I honestly have no idea how to act around Asher he's hot and then he's cold, he's sweet but then he's an ass, and now he knows everything about me and that leaves me vulnerable and I hate that feeling

Asher pops his head in. "Come on."

"Ash I don't feel up to it tonight." "I don't give a shit you've been sitting in this room for weeks now so get the fuck out of bed and come on."

I sigh but drag myself out of bed and follow him out the door. He leads me to his truck and opens my door for me waiting for me to get in before he closes it behind me.

He gets in and starts driving and we both stay silent.

I just stare out the window and watch as the sun slowly starts to set and the darkness succumbs the sky.

I don't realize how long we had been driving until I glance down at my phone and see that 30 minutes have passed.

I look up. "Where are we going?" "You'll see."

I don't push him and turn my attention back towards the window.

I must've dozed off because when I open my eyes we're parked in the middle of a field. I look around to see the drivers seat empty Ashers not in the truck.

I panic and hurriedly climb out. "Good morning sunshine." Asher laughs as I reach the back of the truck to see the truck bed full of pillows and blankets.

"Come here." He reaches his hand out to help me up.

"Why are we here?" I ask getting settled next to him but still keeping myself at a distance.

"Look up."

I turn my attention to the sky and am greeted by a million stars. "This is amazing but why did you bring me here?"

He stays silent just staring at me. I shift uncomfortably. "What?"

He shrugs it off. "Nothing." He lays back and I follow suit.

We stay like this for hours just laying there in silence. I never knew that sitting in silence with someone could be comfortable.

"Whats your story Asher?" I ask still staring at the sky.

"You don't need to have that burden on your shoulders right now." He says.

"Please? I need a distraction." I say hesitantly.

Authors Note

Hey y'all I am so sorry this chapter has taken forever to come out I just recently took on a full time job on top of my other job and so I've been exhausted and in a writers block an haven't been able to figure out how I want this story to develop from here. I know this chapter isn't my best but I wanted to get something out for you guys. If you guys have anything you want to see in the next few chapters, any constructive criticism, etc, please please let me know I so appreciate y'all and want to hear from you! I love seeing y'alls comments and thoughts!

Thank you guys so much for all your support and for being so patient!

chapter twenty six

-------Ashers Pov-------

I sigh after hearing her say that I couldn't deny her. I'd do anything to take her pain away and make her happy even if it means I have to tell her about mine.

"Where do I start?" I laugh half heartedly.

"Your father? My brother told me you didn't have the best relationship with your father." She whispered.

"Me and my dad we used to be incredibly close." I smile at the memories that arise from that single sentence. "My mom was diagnosed with type 4 Leukemia. When the cancer had been discovered it had already spread everywhere there was nothing the doctors could've done. My mom was a saint and so fucking selfless that it was annoying. She never told us if she was in pain before she was diagnosed."

I take a deep breath. "I found her at the bottom of the stairs when I got home from work one day." The words make my eyes start to water but I blink it away refusing to let the tears fall. "She was gone. Her death was ruled a suicide it was said she couldn't deal with the pain anymore but I knew it was my father that drove her to it."

"The second she was diagnosed something snapped in my father. He changed almost overnight. My mother grounded him she was his saving grace and the thought of not having her I think was too much for him to bear. When we brought her home from the hospital after her diagnosis she only became weaker and spent all day in bed. My father hired the best nurses and doctors to be by her side and help with the pain."

I take a deep breath pausing to organize my thoughts.

"While my mother got worst my father grew more and more distant and angry. He drank his days away and often had a revolving door of women in his bed. I had to stay by my mother's side and I tried to keep her from seeing what was happening with my father but it was no use. She knew. She heard the women. She saw them coming and going."

"The day she threw herself down the stairs I believe was one last act of her selfless love for my father. She was letting him go."

"After her death my father was engaged 2 days later to his now wife. I refuse to see them and I refuse to forgive my father no matter how much he begs he does not deserve to be in my life."

The tears suddenly become too much and I can no longer hold them back.

"Oh Ash." Madison grabs me and holds me against her while I sob.

"I'm so sorry." Is all she says over and over to me stroking my hair.

"You didn't deserve to go through any of that."

I relax in her arms I've never allowed myself to cry that much before not even at the funeral. She made me feel safe something I haven't felt in a long time.

I look up at her. "You have such a beautiful kind heart Mads."

She smiles and blushes looking away.

I move her face to look back at me. "Love don't ever hide your face from me." I smile softly at her.

"We're gonna figure this out Mads and you're going to get through all of this I swear to you. You are the strongest woman I know."

I grab her chin and bring her face down closer to mine. I wait for her little nod and my lips finally brush against hers. I groan.

She shifts herself closer to me and I brush my tongue against her lips waiting for her permission. She opens allowing me in. My tongue brushes against her tongue and she moans. That sound could make a man go mad. I sit up and pull her onto my lap. My hands all over her.I can't get enough of her.

I nip at her lips with my teeth "oh Ash." She moans grinding her hips against me.

chapter twenty seven

I wake up with Asher snuggled up against me. Fuck we must've fallen asleep. I look down at my phone to see 17 missed calls from Jake. "Fuck, fuck, fuck." I mutter to myself.

Asher stirs next to me. "Shhh" "Asher wake the fuck up did Jake try calling you?"

"Fuck he called me 30 times." He says looking at his phone. "Did you tell him where we were going?"

"Uhhh..." "Asher what the fuck? We have to go!"

"Fuck he's going to kill me!" Asher mutters to himself as he helps med out of the truckbed.

I call him back. He answers on the first ring. "Mads where the fuck have you been?"

"I'm so sorry Jake I saw that you called. Asher took me to look at the stars to get out of the house and we must've fallen asleep."

"You're with Asher?"

"Uhh yeah." "Why the fuck are you with him alone are you two dating?"

"No of course not don't be like that Jake he was just trying to help."

Asher keeps looking at me with a worried expression on his face.

"Whatever Mads I'll see you when you get home." Is the last thing he says before he hangs up.

"Is he pissed?" Asher asks. I just nod my head.

"Fuck!" Asher punches the wheel causing the horn to go off making me jump.

We ride the rest of the way in silence.

"What happened last night can't happen again." Asher breaks the silence.

"Yeah I know." I turn away from him to face the window so he can't see the hurt on my face.

When we finally pull into the driveway I immediately get out and go inside not waiting for Asher.

I see Jake but I head straight to my room not saying a word.

As soon as I hear the front door open and close I hear Jake and Asher going at it downstairs but I put my headphones in and blast the music trying to block it all out.

---- Ashers POV ----

As soon as I walk in the door and see Jakes face I know shits about to go down.

"Jake don't even start right now man." I try and walk past him but he shoves me back.

"What the fuck is your problem!" I yell pissed off.

"Asher you wanna know what the fuck my problem is its you. It's you taking advantage of my little sister when she's already been through hell she doesn't need you dragging her right back to it!"

"Jake you've got it all wrong I was just trying to help!"

" I don't give a fuck thats not you you're not the fucking nice guy Asher leave my fucking sister alone she doesn't need your shit right now!

"Jake fuck off you have no idea what you're talking about!"

"Yeah what about Ciara?"

Now he's fucking done it. Before I can even stop myself my fist hits his jaw and he's on top of me in seconds throwing punches over and over again I try and get the upperhand but he's throwing punches like a mad man.

I hear Nicky scream and then Noah running down the hall.

"What the fuck is going on get the fuck off of him Jake you're gonna kill him!" Noah yells pulling Jake off of me.

"Asher you okay man?" Noah pulls me to my feet.

"I'm fine." Is all I say before walking off to my room.

I hear Noah questioning Jake as I am leaving.

I pause at Madison's door considering knocking to check on her I raise my fist to do it but decide against it. Jake was right about one thing Madison doesn't need my shit right now. The last thing I want to do is drag her right back to hell.

--- Madison's POV ---

I hear a knock at my door but I ignore it.

"Madison please can I come in?" It's Jake.

"Come in." I can't exactly not let him in no matter how pissed I am this is his house.

"Mads I know you're pissed right now and I apologize for the way I spoke to you on the phone that was uncalled for but I need to talk to you about something."

I nod for him to continue.

"When you were in the hospital I hired a private investigator to do some digging on Cade and he found something."

"Jake why would you do that you need to just drop it they already said it was too late to press charges." I roll my eyes.

"Mads I think we can take him down with a murder charge from what my guy found."

"What are you talking about?"

"He found 2 other ex girlfriends of Cades and both of them after seeing we had some evidence with text messages have agreed to testify against him. He killed one of the girls best friends Mads. They have evidence on it but it was covered up because Cade had his other girl convince her father to bribe the judge so it never even went to trial. My guy found it all and both girls want to see Cade put behind bars and are ready to go to trial when you are."

I take a deep breath. "This is too much Jake."

"I know Mads its a lot to take in but you can think about it you don't have to make a decision now."

"Jake you don't understand you shouldn't have done any of that I can't go to trial I can't relive everything you don't understand the half of went on because you weren't there." I regret those words as soon as they come out when I see the hurt expression on his face.

"I know Mads I'm so sorry I wish I was there that will never stop being my biggest regret but can't you see I'm trying to make up for it?"

"This isn't the way to do that Jake."

www.ingramcontent.com/pod-product-compliance
Lightning Source LLC
Chambersburg PA
CBHW070405200726
48294CB00003B/1093